Charlie's Ghost Town:

the phantom cache

by Ray Golden

ISBN: 0-9774761-2-X

Editor: John Bigler, © 2011 Cover Old West Photo's:
Old Tyme Photography, Manitou Springs, CO

© Back Cover Photo: David Futey
© Cover Design Nicol Ray
©Cover Photo: Keith Ray

Published in the USA by
Books To Believe In
17011 Lincoln Ave. #408
Parker, CO 80134
www.BooksToBelieveIn.com

Proudly Printing by
The Print Connection
www.PrintConnectionDenver.com

ACKNOWLEDGEMENT

I could not begin to write my books without the treasure that I have in my wife Meredith. She works with me every step of the way, one paragraph at a time. She helps me with ideas, editing and most importantly, encouragement. I am the luckiest man alive to have been married to Meredith Bigler Golden for 32 years.

I am also very thankful for my good friend, Dwight Ringler. This book was not possible without him. I want to give him special thanks for offering to carry me off the mountain when I was injured in a fall. He is the only one I know who is strong enough to do it.

Finally, I have to say thanks to Natalie at Black Cat Books in Manitou Springs, Colorado for being the best book signing host I have known.

CHAPTER ONE

Bullets flew through the air on Main Street in the Colorado town of Forest City. Men fell to the ground left and right. George Dillan died in front of Mary O'Malley's Trading Post. Harry Smith slid down from his saddle in front of Little Scott's livery stable. The front windows of Marilyn's General Store exploded as women and children took cover behind the counter. The saloon erupted into a brawl and Sam Starr's outlaw friends decided to join the fray. Hell had broken loose, and Sam was the culprit. Armed with a shotgun and a pistol, he was out to kill as many people as he could. Drunk again, he wanted revenge for being thrown out of town earlier that day. "I'll kill every one of you!" he yelled as he reloaded his guns. "Come on out here for your justice, cowards!"

"Drop those guns or I'll shoot you in the back, you miserable excuse for a husband!" Belle Starr demanded as she rushed out of Fanny Porter's boarding house. She and Sam had been hiding out there from Judge Parker in Fort Smith, Arkansas.

"Go ahead and shoot. I cannot die. I am a Cherokee. The spirit of the Great Bear will protect me from your bullets."

"I'm not fooling around, Sam. Drop those damn guns!" Belle again demanded. Sam turned and fired.

Belle ducked behind a porch beam. Just then, I felt pain in my left ankle. I went down, shot in the foot.

"What's the matter, Charlie? Wake up, wake up, you're dreaming!" My wife pleaded.

"I've been shot, Meredith." I gasped in pain.

"No, Charlie, you haven't been shot. You were dreaming," Meredith assured me.

"If I was dreaming, why does my ankle hurt so much?"

"Oh Charlie, have you been seeing ghosts again?" Meredith asked with deep concern. She was referring to my previous encounters with a ghost named Christiana, whom I'd learned was actually my great, great, great grandmother. I had discovered her past and my own destiny in my search for the lost treasure of Dead Man's Gulch.

"I guess so. I'm sure glad I was dreaming. It all seemed so real. I remember being a whiskey salesman back in the old west. I've always wanted to know what it would be like to actually be there." I replied.

"Yes, Charlie, but you'd better be careful where you go to because you might not be able to get back." Meredith chuckled and rolled over. "Now please go back to sleep, Charlie. Tomorrow's a work day."

"Okay, but my ankle sure feels like that bullet was real," I moaned.

When I awoke the next morning, my ankle was still sore as if the dream was real. I wasn't dissuaded from still wanting to go back to the real old west, though. "Meredith, I want to take Sarah up to Forest City next weekend. I'd like to go into those old buildings to see what's there." Sarah, my Great Pyrenees dog always accompanied me on mountain trips. She'd proven to be valuable on previous trips to Dead Man's Gulch.

"Charlie, haven't you already had enough excitement for one lifetime in all of those trips up to the gulch?" she asked with a smile.

"I guess so, honey, but I can't stop my curiosity." I replied with the boyish grin I wore when I laughed at myself.

Mer said, "Okay Charlie, its fine with me if you go to the mountains and have a look inside those buildings. I guess that's why I married you. Never a dull moment!"

The dream stayed in my memory for several days. Then I had another dream. I found myself strapped into a dental chair. A tall, thin man spoke to me. "You're damn lucky I was in town, stranger. I don't take kindly to strangers who interrupt my poker games. What's your name?" He had a stern edge to his voice.

"Ben. Benjamin Silver," I replied nervously.

"Well Ben, they tell me you're a liquor salesman. If that's true, this here operation is going to cost you one very good bottle of whiskey. Do you agree to my terms?" the man growled.

"But I only have one sample bottle left, sir."

"You only have one left leg too, Ben. Which would you like to keep, the leg or the bottle?" He stared at me with that *I got you* grin on his face.

"I'd like to keep the leg, doctor," I said with definite surety.

"You can call me Doc, Ben. I'm Doc Holliday." He broke into a great big grin.

"But I heard that you were a dentist," I wondered out loud.

"There isn't much difference between pulling teeth or bullets, Ben. Now hold tight," he sneered.

When the bullet had been removed, Doc put it in a jar and looked over at me. He knew I was relieved. "You might want to keep this for a souvenir, Ben. You're a brave man. Now where exactly is that bottle of whiskey?" Doc asked without breaking a single bead of sweat.

"It's over there in my coat pocket, Doc," I replied with relief.

"It was nice doing business with you, Ben. When I find the son of a bitch that shot you, I'll get even for you." His voice had an edge of sincerity.

Suddenly, Meredith woke me with a stir. "Where were you this time, Charlie?"

"Forest City again, I think. I was in a dentist chair and Doc Holliday took a bullet out of my ankle. The year was 1886 on the calendar. I stared at on the wall," I explained.

"Well, I'll say one thing for you Charlie, when you dream, you sure do dream big," she said in amazement.

"But that's the strange thing, Meredith. I don't think I was dreaming. I think I was remembering a past life."

"Now Charlie, you know I've got an open mind, but that's a little hard to believe." She shook her head.

"I'm sure it is hard to believe, but what I'm telling you true. I think my encounters with Christiana have opened some kind of psychic door to my thoughts and I'm having flashbacks of a previous life."

"Okay Charlie, when you put it that way, it makes perfect sense. It's been thundering and lightning tonight. I think we were having a storm the other night when you were dreaming. I wonder if the electricity in the air had anything to do with your dreams," she wondered.

"It could be, Meredith. It feels like a door opens and suddenly I'm there," I described.

"I guess that could be right, Charlie, but please don't get shot again." She wasn't joking.

"Okay, but I don't think I can change what's already happened," I said.

"Go back to sleep now, Charlie. You have one more work day and then you can take your trip to Forest City on Saturday with Sarah," Meredith reassured me.

"That sounds great! I can't wait to go." I released a sigh. The next few days I day dreamed about my upcoming journey. I had one more dream that left me with a dark and scary feeling in my guts. I remembered two brothers who were a part of a large family from old Virginia. I thought they were my brothers. The oldest was Davy. Strong-willed and physical, he led many wagon trains on their way out west in the 1800's. The second brother was Daniel. He was a clever and crafty survivor who had worked as a detective for the Pinkerton agency. I could not remember any more specifics. Toward the end of the dream, one of the brothers was missing; he was there one moment and gone the next. The last thing I remembered was a flash that showed me two men burying something wrapped with oil cloth in a gold miner's hole in the ground and covering the hole with rocks. When they turned, I saw the faces of death, and I shivered from the evil. That feeling of insecurity stayed with me until my other thoughts crowded it to the back of my mind.

CHAPTER TWO

Early Saturday morning, I packed my Jeep with all the supplies experience always told me I might need. Sarah sat patiently at the front door; she always knew when she was going for a ride. I never knew a more intelligent dog. Meredith waited in the hallway and watched to be sure I had everything I needed. Our' cats— Milkbox, Bobo, and Annabelle—wondered what was causing all the commotion. They sat in a row like a king flanked by two princesses. Our one-year-old baby girl, Mariah, sat up on her blanket on the living room floor and smiled at her little kitties. Meredith expressed concern about the weather forecast calling for storms. "There might be thunderstorms up there today. Please be careful and don't take a nap. I don't want you to have any of those dreams up there in the wilderness."

I laughed. "Don't worry about that, I don't think there's any shooting in a ghost town, honey."

"You never know about those things when you're around, Charlie," Meredith said with the wily smile she wore on special occasions.

I drove up Ute pass along with Sarah, her huge, happy head hanging out the rear window. I noticed Aspen trees beginning to turn their famous beautiful gold color. A slight fall breeze was in the Colorado air and few clouds hovered over the crest of Pikes Peak.

Tourists on the highway waved and laughed at Sarah, as they turned off in the direction of Old Colorado City and Garden of the Gods. As was often the case, the temperature cooled by the time we reached Green Mountain Falls. The smell of wood burning in a nearby fireplace permeated the mountain air. I passed several mountain bike riders from the nearby Olympic training center. They struggled mightily to negotiate the steep and curvy road. It would take nearly three hours to arrive at our destination, yet it didn't seem so long with the awesome view afforded to us by the view of the Colorado Rocky Mountains. Over the back of Pikes Peak and past Florissant is a mountain prairie with a view forty miles ahead to the great mountain range of the Continental divide. Florissant is a mountain town known for its dinosaur fossil beds. Sarah barked as we both gazed at a herd of buffalo that were now being bred and raised on a private ranch to the west of Lake George. Elk mingled among the buffalo. I spotted an eagle flying above a rocky knoll with the ease provided by the slight breeze. A short time after, we saw two bighorn sheep enjoying the sun at the top of a nearby rocky hilltop.

When close to Buena Vista, I stopped and gave Sarah a rest. As I let her out of the back of the Jeep, I noticed the remains of a rock slide strewn across the dirt road adjacent to the scenic rest area. "I'm sure glad that we weren't here for that, Sarah," I said to her. It was my habit to talk with her just like she was another person. She thought that she was a real person, too. She acknowledged me by lifting her foot, as if to shake hands. Once back in the Jeep, we continued the final leg of our journey to Forest City.

Arriving at the base of the Mosquito Mountains, I noticed a dirt road with an old wooden sign, which read

Forest City: Last stop before heaven. As I turned off and drove through the thick Aspen trees, an eerie feeling crept over me, as if I was traveling back in time. Previous snow melts had washed out road in many places, and I was pleased to have a vehicle that could negotiate the ups, downs, and holes in the road. The remains of long abandoned railroad tracks tilted on the slope of the adjacent hillside. Now I could see the buildings. Wow, there were fourteen in all!

The first building on the right was a little school building that had a small porch out front and a bell still hanging from its center post. I stopped there first to look around. I found an old wooden sign on the ground. It read *Shelley Dumas School*; I wondered what she was like. I opened the front door to go in, and immediately, I could almost hear the kids laughing. Little furniture was left though, except for a table and two broken chairs. Sarah came in behind me and barked. I followed her out just in time to see a female mule deer and her two button fawns scamper away.

I decided to leave the Jeep parked and walk through town. There wasn't a person anywhere. Sarah and I were alone, yet not lonely; it almost as comfortable as home. We stopped to sit and enjoy the roast beef sandwiches Meredith had packed for us. Yes, Sarah got a sandwich too. I dozed off, but awoke startled from Sarah's loud bark. I saw and heard nothing but knew something was amiss. Sarah must've sensed or heard something. After a few moments of silence, I asked Sarah to come along as we went exploring again.

The next building we came to was the tallest in town. It had three stories, each with porches on the front. The paint had long worn off and an old kerosene lamp lay broken on the front porch next to the remains of a bench. Above the door was a faded carving read *Kathleen Melanson's Boarding House: No snoring.* Somehow I knew she meant it. Going inside, the front desk blocked my entry like a security guard. Dust caked the whole place. An old register was left on a shelf under the top counter. Faded names and dates with room numbers crowded the pages. I thought it might be okay to give this abandoned remnant a home and tucked it inside my backpack. Just then I changed my mind; I sat in the corner and took the book out of the backpack.

My curiosity about who had stayed there got the best of me; I wanted to know! I couldn't read many of the names, but among those I could read on the first page, dated May 5, 1886, were Buck Saybrook, Harvey Clinton, Lisa Putnam, Darlene Danielson, May Summers, Geraldine Ashford, and Dusty Pomfret. An inscription at the top read, "First Day: Heaven help me." As I skimmed through the pages, I recognized names, both famous and infamous: Sam and Belle Starr, Doc Holiday, Leroy Parker, Harry Longabaugh, and Wyatt Earp. Two more familiar names were recorded: Daniel and Davy Silver. That eerie feeling overcame me again, as I noticed writing that looked just like my own. I didn't think anyone could ever write as unique, or badly, as I did, but there it was. The name was Ben Silver. That was the name I'd had in my dreams. How could this be? Was I dreaming again?

At that moment, flashes of lightning sliced through the darkened sky. *Crack! Boom!* The deafening sound of thunder followed the fierce lightning and rain came down hard on the building. Sarah hugged me closer as I shielded her from the onslaught. The hair on both my arms and Sarah's brow stood on end from the electricity in the air. I was surprised at the quickness of the incoming storm. That is the moment that my dreams turned into reality and my reality turned back into the dream.

I felt lonely, but not alone now. Someone else was with me; I was sure of it. As I looked up the staircase, a vision became all too real. A woman was coming down the stairs humming a song. I was astonished! She was dressed in a long, woolen dress edged with lace. An apron hung from her waist. Just then, she looked directly at me. I knew she could see me. "Why are you sitting on the floor, Ben? Your ankle must be hurting. Do you want some help back up to your room?"

Wondering how to get out of this predicament, I got up off of the floor to answer. Then, something truly surreal happened: I became Ben Silver again with his full knowledge. Sarah was still with me and yet with him too. "Hi White Bear, how are you today?" She asked my large, shaggy white dog as she patted Sarah on the head. "Good morning, Kathleen. You're cheery as always this morning. I was just letting White Bear out for her morning break. Yes, my ankle's very sore, but I can make it back up to my room. First I want to go over to Debra Montana's saloon and thank Doc Holiday for taking that bullet out of me."

"Okay Ben, but I'd wait a while if I were you. Doc's in a foul mood this morning. Gizzy Howard tried to cheat him at poker last night and Doc shot him in a duel. Gizzy drew his gun first and Doc shot him while steely-eyed. Sheriff Gary Dawson was sitting nearby and attested to the fairness of the fight. They hauled Gizzy out to Sherman's cemetery this morning and buried his cheating body along with the crooked deck of cards he used. It's a good thing for you that Doc decided to stop at Forest City on his way from Pueblo to Leadville. Doc told me yesterday his good friend Wyatt

Earp was going to stop here and see him on his way to Denver." Kathleen hummed again and walked into the kitchen.

Just then I heard a horse gallop up to the front hitching post. I turned to see what the commotion was just in time to see my brother Daniel rush through the front door. "Ben, are you okay? Jolly Justin stopped by my camp near Leadville last night, and he told me you had been shot by that coward Sam Starr. I was worried as hell, and I hurried over here as fast as I could."

"I just got shot in my ankle. Doc Holiday took the bullet out last night. It's great to see you. I didn't know you were in the area. I thought that you were down Texas way looking for that Bushy Bill?"

"Oh, I caught up with that scoundrel two weeks ago in El Paso and turned him in to those Texas Ranger boys. He'll stretch on a short rope for sure! Word has already gotten out that it doesn't pay to go around shooting Sheriff's deputies in the back," he snickered.

"I'm sure word has gotten out not to have Daniel Silver looking for you either," I added with satisfaction and the pride of a brother.

Daniel put his usual smirk on his face "Well little brother, that was a hard and dusty ride up to this here little town. I would surely like to wet my whistle with some of that top shelf whiskey you have been peddling. I don't suppose there is a sitting place close by for that satisfaction is there?" Daniel queried me the same clever way he used on his suspects.

I grinned knowing what I was about to reveal to the great detective. "There sure is Daniel. Do you remember Debra Montana? We met her in Abilene on our way out west three years ago. She had owned the Silver Star Saloon there."

"Oh sure Ben, how could I forget her! There was never a woman with more spunk than Debra." Daniel tipped his hat to the memory.

"You are sure right," I conceded, as I continued to fill him in. "She sold that saloon after that nasty gunfight with the Sparrow boys and Jess Hatton's family. Her only love, Jess, was killed right out front of her saloon that day and she couldn't stand the memory. She came out here last fall and opened another saloon, just called Debra Montana's Saloon. It is located just up the street. Can you help me hobble on over there?"

"I sure will, Ben. Let's get on over there before you start rambling on for the rest of the day. I never did know anyone who could carry on endlessly with such oratory as you. You should quit that damn liquor selling business and run for public office. Hell, a job like that would be right up square with your tongue twisting abilities. What good is that whiskey business doing for you or anyone else, anyway?" Daniel chuckled at his joke.

"It sure did me a whole bunch of good toward getting Doc Holiday to take that bullet out of my foot." I laughed back. "But, you might have a good idea. I don't guess I'll be able to travel much for a while with this bum ankle of mine. There has been talk around town about electing someone Mayor since there is no such person here now. They say the pay would be $35.00 a month and free room and board at Kathleen's boarding house. Okay Daniel, I'll think it over." I nodded at Daniel, who looked about ready to say something in protest.

Just at that moment I heard a voice behind me. "No need to think it over Ben, I'll put it to a vote with the citizen's committee this very evening." Scott Curly had been walking behind us. He owned Little Scott's Livery

Stable and was head of the citizen's committee. He continued, "You're brother is right Ben. You are a silver tongue devil and would represent us well in the Capitol of Denver. You would be a shoe in. Will you accept?"

"Well I-" I started to respond, but Daniel broke in to the conversation.

"He'll take the job, if you throw in a pair of six shooters and a fast horse. That old mule of his isn't going to get the job done." Daniel stared down Scott after his interruption.

"We will surely agree to those terms," Scott conceded as he walked across the street toward Clyde's Barber Shop. As he got over to the other side of the street, he yelled back over to me. "I'll let you know how the vote goes."

Daniel picked up the conversation. "You see that, little brother. All you have to do is walk down the street with me, and I can get you into a job." White Bear started barking at us. She had been walking with us, as she never let me out of her sight. "I see you still have your best buddy, Ben. What is she excited about?"

"I think that she smells those great biscuits Debra makes every day," I replied matter-of-factly.

"Well, let's get on in there little brother." Daniel smiled and slapped me on the back.

"Okay, oh look at that!" I spotted a penny upturned in the dirt and reached down to pick it up, while grinning the wide grin that always accompanied finding money. It was a fine, shiny 1886 penny.

"Ben, I can't believe you. You have been finding money since you were a little boy," Daniel shook his head and laughed.

As I packed it into my pocket, I had a second thought. "Daniel, I am thinking that this here penny might give one of us good luck some day. I'm going to put it in this crack in this horse post in case you or I need it some day."

"That sounds great Ben, good thinking." Daniel smirked while I wedged the penny into the crack.

A stage coach raced into town and stopped right in front of Debra Montana's saloon. Some happy children ran by as they were playing a wagon wheel race game. I heard three other children rooting from Carol Sergeant's porch. Their names were Landon, Ellie and Sadie. The racers were in three sets of two, each set rolling a wheel with a stick through the center, trying to get to the finish line first. They yelled, "Go Caitlin, go Kolby." And then from another, "Go Lindsey, go Ashley." And then from the third bystander I heard, "Go Braiden, go Kaylee." A well-dressed and -groomed man stepped out of the coach and walked into the saloon hollering to Debra with an eastern accent. "Here's your poster, for Kellie's show tonight. We'll be expecting payment after the show!"

Daniel and I grinned at each other with anticipation and looked back at the coach. Inside, we could see an attractive woman wearing a feathered hat. "Could that possibly be Kellie Repute, Daniel?" My excitement must have been evident.

"Sure enough is, Ben! I saw her show in Santa Fe. She is a mysterious woman but quite talented. I hope she sings "Build Me a Home" tonight. That's my favorite. I had a chance to talk with her that evening at the famous Holly's Hotel. She is very well-spoken and a delight to admire." Daniel motioned for me to follow him to the coach. "Well hello Kellie. It's been a long trail since I met you in Santa Fe. How are you?"

"Well, just fine Mister Daniel Silver. I wouldn't forget your handsome face. I sure am glad that you still have your skin, considering the dangerous life that you lead." Kellie said.

"So am I Kellie." Daniel smiled and lifted his well worn hat. "I would like to ask if you would honor us with your presence at dinner." He nodded to me. "We can celebrate my skin being in place." We all laughed.

"I would be most delighted to enjoy a dinner with you and your brother. I am very pleased to make your acquaintance Ben." She held out her hand and curtseyed. I had never met a lady with a more dignified greeting.

"It is my complete delight to meet such a talented, famous, and might I add beautiful singer." As I complimented her, I sensed a slight blush in her already rosy cheeks.

Daniel picked up where I left off. "That Ben sure does have a way with words Kellie, but he hits his mark in a most accurate fashion."

"Well, I surely do thank and admire both of you gentlemen as well. I will be staying at Kathleen Melanson's Boarding House this evening. Can we meet in her dining room before the show? Say 7 P.M.?" Her feminine tone had just the slightest bit of flirtation.

As I nodded yes, Daniel replied with a lift of his hat and a nod of his own. As the coach left, Daniel looked over at me and said, "Let's get that drink now little brother."

"That sounds great to me handsome one." I chuckled at my joke. "Are you thirsty White Bear?" She jumped up and down in her usual way of knowing that a treat was in the offing. Then we turned toward the swinging doors to Debra Montana's Saloon and made our entrance.

CHAPTER THREE

As we entered, the chatter of many conversations greeted us, but none of the patrons even so much as paused. Seated at the first table, I heard four miners celebrating their find of what must have been a fair amount of gold. I overheard one of them bursting with excitement. "I told you guys months ago that we should have started our search up on Kenosha Pass! Now, maybe you'll be listening to me!"

A second miner retorted, "Oh yah Earl. That was surely the first time you have ever been right about anything in your whole live long life."

Earl shot back, "Say what you want Bob Evans, but who found all that there gold in yer sack?" The other two scruffy men almost fell out of their chairs laughing.

As I looked to the bar, Debra was laughing and joking with a couple of cowboys. When she looked up and recognized us, she put her hands on her hips and a half-amazed, half-amused look on her face. "Well I'll be hog tied! I am always at a loss for words when I look upon you two handsome gentlemen. Hello, White Bear, did you come in for one of my famous biscuits?" As we grinned from the compliment, Debra continued the one-sided conversation. "Why don't you sit at my favorite table with me over here next to the window? I'll get White Bear a treat and be right with you."

After we sat down, the bartender, Holly, asked what we'd like to drink. "What will your poison be today, Ben? We have a special called the Bullet Chaser." That made everyone at the bar laugh as they knew I had been shot. Holly was a jokester. She was working as a bartender just to have something to do. She had a good nest egg now after selling her hotel.

I quipped back, "I'll have one have one of those Golden brew beers, funny girl."

"Yah, give me one too, and a shot of that top shelf whiskey Ben has been selling to you," Daniel added as he doffed his hat and winked at Holly.

Just as Debra joined us, Joe Hensmith, the editor of the *Mountaineer*, came running in. "Hey boys," he huffed, "I wanted to let you know that the mail rider just came into town with a letter for me. I have it here. It's from my friend Harvey Milk at the *Colorado Springs Gazette*. He wrote your brother Davy had just come into town there with nearly 40 wagons in tow from Abilene! That sure is quite a wagon master you have for a brother there, traveling through that dangerous Indian Territory without an Army escort." A sense of admiration shone through his heavy breathing.

"Let me read that." Daniel grabbed hold of the letter. "Sure enough Ben. It looks like our older brother surely does have nine lives."

"Yah, he'll never change. He's been looking after the welfare of others just like he'd always done for us while we were being reared up." I said in admiration and pride for my oldest brother who had been leading wagon trains west for five years with never a wagon lost.

"That gives me a good idea. I wonder if he could lead those settlers up here. We sure do need a growing town, and it's a good place for them to settle with all the recent gold finds." Debra's eyes widened at the thought.

Joe immediately jumped into the conversation. "That is a brilliant idea Debra! What do you boys say about sending a message to Davy in Colorado Springs with the rider? We can probably still catch him; I think he is over at Marilyn's store getting supplies."

Daniel said quickly, "Let me have that letter and a pencil Joe. I'll write the reply for him to give to Davy." As Daniel began writing, he spoke the words. "Davy, this is your brother Daniel. Ben and I are in Forest City. Park County is just west over Pikes Peak from Colorado Springs. Ben has been shot in the foot and cannot travel. We would like to see you, as it has been quite a long time. This little town is a good place for those pilgrims to settle. There's gold in them thar hills and game and fertile fields aplenty. Could you make haste with those settlers up to this lovely spot?"

"Excellent! That'll bring him Daniel." The surety in my voice shone through.

"Well, let's celebrate gentlemen! Where are those drinks, Holly?" Debra exclaimed. Joe ran out with the letter and whistling a joyful tune. Holly set the drinks on the table with a big smile on her face. The first big gulp of that golden beer cooled our tongues and excited our taste buds. The piano player struck up a pleasant tune and a young Ute Indian squaw hurried to the table bringing some mouth-watering biscuits for us. Her stunning beauty caught my attention. With olive skin and long, black flowing hair, she moved with the grace of a bird in flight. "Ben, this is Maipaa. She was given her name, friendly water, because she was born next to a well-protected pond with many beautiful fish. A stray bullet from a Deer Lake skirmish between the

Ute Indians and a band of outlaws injured her, and I have nursed her back to health. She stays with me now and says she will never leave my side."

"She is assuredly the most delightful looking woman I have ever seen, Debra." I turned my attention to Maipaa. "I am very pleased to meet you. Do you speak English?"

Her clear English surprised me. "Hello, Mister Ben. I am happy to know you. Your dog is a powerful spirit and very beautiful."

"She means the Ute Indians worship the Bear, Ben." Debra clarified and then spoke to Maipaa. "This other gentleman is Ben's brother Daniel."

Maipaa greeted Daniel with a smile and a bow of the head. As she walked away, I felt taken with her and admired her walk back to the kitchen. This did not escape Daniel's attention. "Little brother, I've never seen you look at a woman quite that way." At this I blushed and smiled at him and Debra.

"Daniel, that's probably because I've never seen a woman quite like her! She took my breath away." I replied after catching my breath. Just then, as Maipaa passed the side door to the alley, I could see Gizzy Howard's older brother Lloyd sneak in carrying a shotgun and begin to look around from the shadows of a darkened corner. I recognized his target at the same moment Lloyd spotted him and lurched toward an adjoined room. In the small poker room sat Doc Holiday with three other men at his table. I yelled, "Look out Doc! He has a shotgun!" Daniel recognized the danger and jumped to his feet, drawing his six-shooter so fast his right hand was a blur. He fired two shots as Lloyd looked over and raised his shotgun to silence me; Doc jumped up and fired his Colt revolver without a moment's hesitation. Lloyd jolted back toward the door; his shotgun flew backward into the air with him. He hit the door with a loud thud and slid slowly to the floor, his eyes rolling upward. He was most decidedly dead. Complete silence replaced the din of the saloon. Daniel sat back down and drained another sip of whiskey as if nothing had happened. Doc looked over at me and Daniel with a smirk of satisfaction that quickly became a very rare smile, which he followed with a tip of his hat. Debra ordered drinks for everyone. White Bear investigated Lloyd to be sure the threat was gone. Maipaa returned quickly to our table and placed her hand on my shoulder as if to say that she was glad that I was safe. I placed my hand on her hand as if to say that I was also glad that I was safe, and I surely was.

Doc announced the end of the poker game, picked up his chips, and strode to our table. "Well Ben, it would appear I am now in your debt." He shifted his attention to Daniel. "Stranger, I don't know many people with a quicker draw than me, but I'm glad you showed up."

"This is my brother Daniel." I said and grinned with pride for my brother's talent with a gun.

"I'm much obliged for your fast draw Daniel. Now, I know my reputation may not be the greatest, but rest assured I am loyal to my friends, which I now consider both of you."

Before either of us could respond, the front doors swung open, and a tall stranger confidently strutted toward us. Once at our table, he addressed Doc. "Doc, I thought you were going to take it easy after that little dust up we had at the OK corral."

"That surely was my intention Wyatt. I guess trouble just follows me. These two new friends of mine are Daniel and Ben Silver. They have just come to my rescue from that back- shooting son-of-a bitch lying on the floor over there."

"Well, in that case, I would like the honor of buying a drink for the two strangers who have provided such able support for my friend. You can count on my friendship as well." Wyatt addressed us with the ease of a life-long companion.

"Will you join us Wyatt?" queried Daniel as he pulled back a chair. "It would be nice to have another lawman in with this bunch of rascals."

"Yes, please do!" I added, noting the gun skills of my three companions.

"I would be my pleasure to have a drink with you," Wyatt replied as he sat down and wiped his brow. "It's been a dusty ride up this hill. Is that you Debra Montana?" He turned his attention to the female at the table. "Pardon my manners for not addressing you sooner."

"It sure is Wyatt. How nice of you to remember me! It's been some time since our Dodge City days!"

"It has been too long to suit me Debra. What do you have in that kitchen for a hungry traveler?" Wyatt queried.

"How does an elk steak sound to you?" Debra motioned toward the kitchen.

"Sounds like I came to the right kitchen!. I would love some of your best recipe beans and two of those famous biscuits." Wyatt's look of satisfaction quickly disappeared and his voice shifted from playful to serious as he focused on Doc. "Who was that coward that tried to shoot you in the back, Doc?"

"That was Lloyd Howard. His brother Gizzy tried to cheat me and drew on me last night when I called his bluff. I dispatched him quick, and he is buried with that damn cheating deck of cards! Now, we are rid of both of them no good brothers!" Doc finished his sentence with his whiskey glass to his lips.

White Bear came over to the table to sniff Wyatt. "I have never seen a dog this big! She sure is friendly." Wyatt grinned and patted White Bear's head.

"She knows the difference between a good guy and a bad guy; she isn't nearly as friendly to the bad guys!" I beamed with pride for my companion. "She has come to my rescue many times. There is nothing, save a grizzly bear, that could challenge her and win." The swinging doors opened again, and to my surprise it was our oldest brother Davy! Our father wanted us to be reputable men when we grew up; he named us after three major contributors to Americana: Davy Crockett, Daniel Boone, and Ben Franklin. I yelled out, "Davy, we're over here!"

Davy rushed over to our table and said in a flurry, "Hi Daniel. Ben, are you all right? I heard down in Colorado Springs you had been shot. I rode directly up here to check on you!"

"I'm okay Davy. I just got shot in the ankle. News sure does travel fast in these parts! We just sent a letter to you with the mail. I doubt you'll be back in Colorado Springs to receive it!" We all chuckled at the irony.

"Joe Hartley, the train conductor, told some friends about the shooting in the saloon I was in last night. I just came in from Kansas way leading 40 wagons full of settlers. Where is that murderous Sam Starr?" Davy asked. "I'll take care of that business right now."

"I would have gone for him today, if that coward hadn't already run for cover." Daniel said.

"You guys let me settle with him when my chance comes around." Doc said getting in to the conversation.

"No wait just a minute. I'd like to make sure his

head feels the butt end of my gun first." Wyatt said and everyone laughed. "I'll take it that this here big man is another brother of you two."

"You got that right." Doc said. "Hello Davy, I met you over Kansas City way on my way out west."

"Oh sure Doc, I remember. You silenced that big baby of a man with a toothache." Davy said.

"Doc, you didn't shoot him, did you?" Wyatt asked with eyes wide open.

"No Wyatt, but I most certainly would have if he didn't stop his whining." Doc replied with that steely eyed grin. Davy sat down with us just as Debra brought out a plate full of elk steaks, a bowl of beans, and a big basket of biscuits.

Maipaa followed Debra out of the kitchen with a fresh bandage for my ankle. Maipaa sat down on that floor and began to change the bandage for me, all the time smiling in a nurturing kind of way. Davy said to me in that deep, strong voice, "Well Ben, it would appear that your brothers need not worry any longer about your shot up foot. It would seem that this young lady has that well in hand. Who might she be, Ben?"

"I think I may have just acquired a new best friend, brother. This is Maipaa. She is from the Ute Indian tribe. Debra Montana, the owner of this saloon, came to the rescue of Maipaa. Debra nursed her back to health from a wound, and now Maipaa is fully dedicated to her." I told him.

"It appears to me that this lady is also very dedicated to you too, Ben." Davy said as he turned his attention to Debra. "Might you be part of the Montana family from down Petersburg way?"

"Yes Davy, you are right. Do I know you?"

"No, I don't believe so. I sure do know a Robert Montana, however. Might he be a relative of yours?"

Davy asked her.

"Yes, he's my brother. Is he well? How do you know him?" Debra asked.

"He sure is well. He rode with my party of wagons from Topeka to Colorado Springs. He was a mighty handy rider to have along about two weeks ago when we were attacked by a Kiowa war party. He single handedly killed several of those painted terrors. I new saw a man who could shoot so straight with a pair of pistols. I am in debt to him and very happy to make your acquaintance. If I can accommodate any particular needs which you may have, I would be grateful to be at your service." Davy said with much sincerity.

"Thank you so much. The comfort that you have just given me of my brother's welfare shall be quite enough, I am sure." Debra said in relief. "Did he say where he was going to, Davy?"

"Well, yes ma'am, he sure did. He said that he was heading back up to these here mountains to get his fill of beaver pelts." Davy said.

"Oh, I hope he comes by this way. I would like to see him." Debra wished out loud. "Aren't you two going to try some of this food?" She glared at me and Daniel.

"Thanks Debra, but we have a dinner date with Kellie Repute this evening." Daniel said.

Then I had an inspiring thought. "Daniel if it's all the same to you, I'll take this pretty woman to dinner and you can have dinner by your lonesome with Kellie." I looked at Maipaa, as she bowed in agreement.

"Okay Ben, it would appear that for a change you have led me down the garden path." Daniel said as he grinned wide.

Everyone around the table laughed. That was the moment that the front doors swung open and in walked four of the nastiest looking men I had ever seen. They looked over to our table and sneered viciously. "Where is the damn bartender? We'll be having us a drink and we aren't in a mood to be waiting." The tallest man said sharply. He wore a holster swung around his chest and under one arm ready for quick use. His eyes were black and cold. He appeared to be the leader of that nasty looking bunch.

As they headed off to a table in the far corner, Debra whispered to us. "That is young Johnny Reynolds. He is trouble for sure. Those other men with him must be his gang. I heard just the other day from Joe Hensmith that they might be headed this way. His father Jim Reynolds and his Uncle John were the leaders of the Reynolds gang. Back in the 1864 they robbed many a honest gold miner and rancher up in these parts. It is rumored that they were trying for loot for the Confederacy. The story goes that they and a large gang pulled off many robberies in these parts before they were finally confronted by a posse over on the other side of Kenosha Pass. They say that Jim and John had just buried over $60,000 in cash and two cans of gold dust weighing twenty pounds, the afternoon before the shooting began. Most of that bunch escaped the posse before they met their destiny elsewhere. But, it has been said that the loot is still buried in an old prospector's hole. They stuck a knife into a tree close by and broke off the handle to point the way. Joe said those boys might have gotten hold of a map and are going up there to find that cache. It won't be easy to find. Joe also said a forest fire three years ago likely burned down that tree with the pointing knife. You men be sure to mind your back around them critters," Debra cautioned.

"I just came over Kenosha Pass last evening." Wyatt said. Saw the strangest thing. I set up my camp next to a swampy area and got a good fire going. After a while I saw someone riding by on a horse, but I could not really see his face. I yelled out yonder to him but there was no answer in return."

"Wyatt, if that was who I think, then you didn't see his face because he didn't have one." Debra said with wide eyes.

"Whatever do you mean, Debra, no face?" Wyatt quizzed her.

"Harvey tells of one of them outlaws who got killed to have had his head removed by a doctor in a posse. He kept that head in a jar. It is in his office even until today. That place you were at is called Phantom trail because that headless outlaw rides the trail looking for his loot-or his head." Debra laughed.

"Well, I would not have believed it if I didn't see it with my own eyes." Wyatt replied.

"Wyatt, I don't believe in them apparitions. But, I sure would not presume to question the word of such a friend as you. So, I will give you the benefit of the doubt and defend your story till the last," Doc insisted.

Davy, Daniel and I just nodded our heads. "We have all seen a ghost at our farm in Virginia when we were kids. It was in the barn and we had seen that ghost whenever it was storming. None of us wanted to be the one whose turn it was to feed the animals on a night like that. That poor man must have been hanged in that barn. You could sometimes see him swinging in there from the rafter. We didn't stick around long enough to look much." I said as I spoke for all three of us.

"That reminds me of a rustler we once knew down Tombstone way, hey Wyatt?" Doc said to Wyatt with a coy smile.

"Sure does Doc, wonder how that happened to that poor man," Wyatt replied with an equally coy smile as if they had a private joke we couldn't get in on but could make a pretty good guess.

"Bartender, I said we wanted a drink!" Johnny yelled out to Holly who was just returning from the kitchen.

"Be there in a minute," Holly replied.

"You'll bring us a drink right this here minute or I'll be putting a bullet in your back side," Johnny warned.

"Now, hold your patience Johnny Reynolds!" Debra warned him with a yell over. "This is my establishment and there will be no such talk here. You can be civil mannered here or you can leave now."

"Just who do you think you are talking to us that way?" Johnny barked out.

"She'll be Debra Montana. Now you had better behave sonny," Doc growled at him.

"Oh yah and who might you be? You talk pretty tough but you look pretty scrawny to me," Johnny asked in a condescending manner.

"That would be Doc Holiday—and sir to you sonny boy—and my name is Wyatt Earp. Now I suggest that you boys do as Ms. Montana says, and you won't be a flying out of here on your back side," Wyatt chastised him.

"I am not afraid of you lawman, the Doc neither. I got three of the fastest guns from the New Mexico territory right here with me. Jack Thorpe right there in black and Jesse and Billy Hayes right there too. Are you two challenging us to the street?"

"We five will be happy to give you a boot out to the street." Daniel stood up with an eye of indignation.

"Who might you other boys be?" Jack Thorpe questioned him.

"We three here are the Silver brothers and we had our fill of punks like you. Make your play anytime you wish," Davy stepped in. Now, all five of us were standing at the ready.

Johnny grabbed hold of Thorpe's hand and said, "We are outnumbered, we'll make this stand another time."

Billy Hayes stood up with Jesse as he said, "Hell, we don't need to drink around them anyhow, Johnny. Let's go across the street, and we'll be seeing them another time."

"Yah Johnny, we can take them down anytime we want," Jesse commented with a false bravado as they all walked back toward the door and out with a final smirk.

"I almost got shot twice in two days," I said while handing another biscuit to White Bear.

"Ben, if you weren't such a peaceful man, I believe you would be the fastest man with a gun anywhere," Daniel commented.

"You better believe it friends, I've seen him clear leather when we were young, that is still the fastest I have ever seen," Davy said nodding his head.

"I'm glad that I didn't know that last night. I might not have been so persistent to take that last bottle of whiskey from him," Doc winked, and everyone broke out roaring with a laugh.

"Come with me Davy. I'll get you a room at Kathleen's boarding house." I waved at Davy.

"Hey, wait for me. I will need a room too," Daniel said.

We said our goodbyes to Doc, Wyatt and Debra and headed out for the boarding house. What a great feeling it was to be with my brothers again. Just at the moment we walked out onto the boardwalk, little Scott Curly approached us and yelled out at me, "Whoopee Ben! We just elected you the mayor of this soon to be great town. It was a unanimous first vote, and we all were in certain agreement. We would be proud to have you represent us in the capitol city of Denver, and we know you will help our fine town grow and prosper. Now, the arrangements have already been made for you to pick out the horse of your own choosing down at my stable; I'll give a bargain price for the town to pay. We also voted to pay Marilyn's general store the advertised price for any pair of six shooters and holster that you choose at your convenience. Your pay will be thirty five dollars per month, plus expenses and room and board, if that would be okay with you."

"Thank you, Scott. I whole heartedly accept your generous offer. I will repay your compliments with a genuine attention to my duties and affection for this great settlement called Forest City," I responded.

"Wow Davy, can that brother of ours say some eloquent words, or am I just smitten with the prospect of pride in a brother?" Daniel exclaimed.

"He sure as hell can, Daniel. Do you remember the time when we were young, and farmer John Addison caught us taking an apple each from his apple tree behind his barn. Ben just explained to him that we just needed some energy to surprise him with us volunteering to clean out his chicken coop. From then on, he said it would be fine to take an apple each any time we wanted," Davy said with a big smile.

"Yes, I sure do Davy. I also remember the smell of our boots for a long time after," Daniel said as we all laughed.

Little Scott followed with a giggle, "Well, you three brothers, I don't have an apple tree. But, you can all come and clean my barn any time you wish." And then he walked away, chuckling all the way down Main Street.

CHAPTER FOUR

The sun was beginning to set over the still snow-covered Mosquito mountain range as we got closer to Kathleen's boarding house. A slight breeze glided past us from Heaven's Hill to the west of the town. Our mood was soaring with the wind like an eagle in its glory. We all realized what a tremendous gift it was from high to have been given a family such as we were. "Have you guys heard from our two sisters or those other two brothers?" Davy asked us.

"I got a letter in Abilene from Gary," Davy said. "He wrote that Ma and Pa took a trip to Richmond to see a doctor to get the shrapnel removed from Pa's back that he had been carrying around since the battle of Little Round Top at Gettysburg. He said that the shrapnel had been moving and causing great pain in his back. The operation went well, and Pa is spunkier than ever now."

"If that is truly the case, then it is a darn good thing for those Yankees that the fighting has stopped," Daniel said with total confidence.

I added, "Yah, do you remember the story about Pa going up against three Yankee soldiers and a mule and only left the mule standing?"

"Yah, he said he was happy to take the mule prisoner to carry his gear," Davy chuckled.

As we all laughed, Daniel added, "I remember Ma saying that she knew that was a Yankee mule the minute Pa brought it home after the war. Darndest, stubbornest mule she ever saw. She couldn't get it to plow one single patch for corn!"

That was the moment that we spotted three riders galloping into town and stop in front of Fanny Porter's saloon. Those four ruffians that we had words with at Debra's saloon came out to meet them. They began to talk to each other and then they all looked over at us. "I think we might have a little trouble with those boys," Daniel sneered.

"I haven't seen seven ruffians yet, that we couldn't take," Davy reassured. "If they get any more friends though, we might want to get Pa out here."

"You aren't just kidding, Davy," I said with a chuckle. "Those boys would surely high tail it as soon as they heard he was coming." White Bear growled over at that rabble and straightened her back. She had a sense for that type of man and would surely defend me with her very life. "It's okay White Bear," I said to her. "Just keep an eye on them."

Davy looked over at White Bear and said to me, "Ben, I wouldn't want to challenge her. She has been looking after you since you got her back in '81."

"She saved my back side at Hoosier Pass from a hungry pack of wolves. She fought them like a crazed grizzly! They all ran away yelping in pain in just a very short time. She is very gentle if you are on her good side, but I'll tell you this, the wolves surely have regretted getting on her bad side-and my back side," I said to my brothers with wide eyes and a grateful heart.

As we walked into Kathleen's front door, Davy said to me, "Well, let's get your back side into your room, so you can get ready for dinner with that very attractive Indian woman who seems to have your fancy."

"I think he's in love Davy. I've never seen him look like that before," Daniel teased.

"Well, you guys might be right. You just might be." I assured them with my own tease.

"Hello Ben, how is your ankle doing? And who are these two handsome gentlemen?" Kathleen asked with enthusiasm from behind the front counter.

"I can live with it, Kathleen. These two handsome gentlemen are my brothers." I grinned and added, "This is handsome Davy, and this is most definitely handsome Daniel."

"Okay Ben. That will be quite enough promoting for today. You've already been appointed mayor of this town. Please don't get us elected for anything," Daniel quipped.

"We would like a room for the evening Miss Kathleen. It is a pleasure to know such a gracious hostess," Davy said, taking the lead.

"I have two very nice rooms available across the hall from Ben, upstairs. Kellie Repute has also just checked into a room up there. You'll have an enchanting neighbor." Kathleen winked at me with a blush on her pretty face.

"We'll take them," Daniel quickly said. "How much money do you need for a night?"

"Fifty cents includes breakfast in the morning. Two bits more will get you a bath and a shave. It looks like you gentlemen could use both after being on the trail."

"Here is two dollars Miss Kathleen. It is Miss, isn't it?" Davy asked while handing over the shiny new coins.

"Well, yes it is Davy, and how sweet of you to ask." Kathleen blushed again.

"Well then, Miss Kathleen, might I be bold enough to ask for your company this evening for dinner?" Davy asked smoothly.

"I would be delighted to keep your company in my dining room this evening Mister Davy Silver. Let me show you to your rooms." Kathleen picked up two keys and started climbing the stairs, while holding up the bottom of her dress so as not to trip.

Daniel pulled me up by the left arm. "Come on little brother, I'll give you a strong shoulder to lean on."

"You always have, Daniel." I praised him for always being there for me.

At the very moment that we all reached the top of the stairs, gunshots rang out on the street. First three shots, then two more. Then we heard that voice I had remembered so well. It was Sam Starr, back for more killing. "Come back out here for some more justice, you cowards. I am not done with you yet." He growled. I had then realized he must have snuck back into town without anyone knowing. We all went to the hall window and looked outside onto the street. Sure enough, it was the outlaw who had shot me.

Just as Daniel said, "I'll go down and take care of that snake in the grass," Wyatt Earp and Doc Holiday stepped out from Debra's Saloon and squared off in the street with Starr.

Wyatt spoke first. "Drop them pistols or take your last breath."

Sam hollered back, "Who are you brave man!"

Wyatt snarled back, "They call me Wyatt, Wyatt Earp."

"It matters none to me Earp! I have heard of you and would have killed you sooner or later anyhow. I don't like lawmen!" Sam barked out.

Then Doc spoke up. "Leave him to me Wyatt. He interrupted my poker game and shot Ben."

"And who might you be?" Sam queried.

"My name is Doc, Doc Holiday. You can call me Mister Holiday." Doc's eyes glared through Sam.

"I'll call you Mister dead Holiday in a moment." Sam threatened while lifting his pistol.

Doc was as fast as the wings of a hummingbird. A single shot rang out from his shooter as Sam fell forward and to the ground with a bullet right between his eyes. Everyone watching gasped with the incredible moment of daring. Doc walked over to Sam to be sure that he was dead and looked up at us through the window and yelled, "I promised to take care of that son-of-a-bitch for you. It would appear that I have done just that, Ben. You owe me another bottle of that good whiskey whenever you can get one."

"I'll buy that bottle for you, Doc, and I'll be bringing it back from the best saloon in Colorado Springs in a few days." Davy yelled out with satisfaction and much appreciation for my avenger.

Then suddenly, we heard the clapping of a runaway buckboard. Into town it came with dust clouding the street. A young woman aboard was screaming, "Sheriff Kinney, Sheriff Kinney, where is the Sheriff? They murdered my brother."

Clyde yelled out from his barber shop, "The sheriff is in Leadville."

Wyatt walked quickly over to the buckboard and spoke to her, "Now young lady, calm down. What has happened to set you off in such a way?"

"They murdered my brother, Jeremy. Three men shot him. I saw them shoot him at the creek below Kenosha Pass and ride off in this direction," she said excitedly.

"What is your name young lady?" Wyatt asked.

"Sue Rogers; they call me Saint Louis Sue!" she exclaimed.

"Well Sue, let me help you down off of that buckboard and we'll see how we can help you. Let's go over to Kathleen's boarding house and get you a chair and a drink." Wyatt helped her down.

We all went back down the stairs to the dining room to meet Sue and hear her story. Kathleen quickly made a pot of coffee and we all sat down at the table around this tearful lady. Daniel spoke to Sue first. He said, "Sue, my name is Daniel Silver. I am a detective for the Pinkerton Agency. Can you tell me where you were, what happened, and if you can identify those murderous men?"

"Yes, Jeremy and I were traveling here to Colorado from St. Louis. Jeremy had Consumption and we had heard that the climate here was suitable for such a condition. We were on our way to Forest City to settle down. I am a seamstress, and my cousin Aaron told me that many families were moving to this lovely town in the Rocky Mountains. I supposed that this would be a good place for me to make a living and support Jeremy and me. We arrived at Kenosha Pass and rode down the Phantom Trail to a beautiful mountain lake to spend the night. Last night was the scariest evening I have ever spent in the outdoors. We continued to hear a horse walking nearby and snorting. At one moment we had seen that horse with a rider who appeared not to have a head. We thought about leaving there immediately. But, my stubborn brother Jeremy, bless his spirit, insisted that there weren't no headless horseman on this earth that could chase him anywhere. This morning, we were doing some gold panning in the little river that empties into the lake.

Jeremy let out a hoot as he came up with a pan full of gold dust. It was then, at that moment that the shots rang out. Jeremy went down quickly into the stream. I looked up to see those three men. They were dressed in long coats and water stained hats. There was a chestnut horse and two back stallions. The men all had beards. They looked at me and fired more shots over my head and then turned and rode away quickly. I dragged Jeremy's body to the wagon and rode quickly here." She seemed exhausted as she finished.

Davy quickly jumped into the conversation. "Sue's description of those men sounds to me like the riders who came to town earlier and met with the Reynolds gang."

Kathleen added, "I saw those riders, seven of them I think, sneaking out of town by the lower gulch behind this building not to long ago."

Wyatt took the lead. "Who will come with me to question those men?"

Daniel spoke up first. "I will most certainly go Wyatt. It is almost dark now. I can track them better in the daylight. Why don't we leave first thing in the morning, and we can catch up to those varmints."

"You can count on me and my guns," added Doc calmly.

Davy followed, "Count me in, too; I'm a fair hand with my six shooters."

Daniel turned to Davy and sighed, "Thanks Davy, I would sure like your company. But I am sure we can handle those men. It might be best if you could get your settlers up to this place and finish your job."

"I guess you have a good point there Daniel. I'll be back in a couple days if you need me."

Wyatt reassured Davy, "We'll keep your brother's back clear of trouble."

I offered my help too. "Let me pick out some guns and go with you all."

Daniel said, "Ben, I think you might slow us down with that foot all shot up. You might do us the most good if you can contact Matt Baker at the Pinkerton Agency in Colorado City and ask him to dispatch my good friends Steve Clark and Nate Gang to assist in the capture of those ruffians."

"Okay Daniel, as you wish, but gosh darn it, could you please be careful," I insisted.

The side door opened then and in came Deborah and Maipaa with some food they had prepared. Kellie Repute came down the stairs and said hello. We all enjoyed a very nice feast instead of the quiet dinners we had planned. After dinner, Maipaa once again showed her compassion for me by changing the bandage on my ankle. I was feeling an inescapable admiration and unmistakable feeling of love for her. Kellie Repute was ready to perform now at Deborah's saloon, and we all followed her there to enjoy the best performance any of us had ever seen. She sang a song called "Build me a home" in a most heartfelt way. After the show everyone went to their rooms, except for Maipaa. She insisted that she stay with me to take care of my foot. Well, I supposed that I really didn't have much choice. So I most certainly said okay. My foot was feeling much better after a while.

I awoke to Joe Peterson's dog barking from out behind his miner supply store. Maipaa looked out the window to see what the commotion was. "Go back to sleep Ben. It is just a mule deer and her two fawns passing by on their way to the river for a drink of water."

I quickly replied, "I think my ankle is hurting again. Why don't you come back to bed."

She kindly complied with my wish. "Maybe we should get our own teepee together Ben. I should always take care of you."

That is when the words spilled from my mouth. "Okay Maipaa, when I get settled in as the mayor of this little town we can get married, if you want to."

"Oh yes Ben, I will make you very proud." She smiled her beautiful smile.

The streets of the town came more alive after a while. From my window I could hear people laughing and kids playing. As I looked out the window, I could see Marilyn out in front of her store with some friends. I could hear her talking about special dishes that were due to arrive any day. Clyde was sitting on the front porch of his barber shop, waiting for his first customer. Little Scott was feeding the horses in front of his stable, and Debra was sweeping the front porch of her saloon. Kellie Repute was saying goodbye to Daniel in front of her coach while Davy was saddling his horse. "Let's go out and say goodbye to my brothers." I beckoned to Maipaa.

"Yes Ben, we must always wish good fortune to those we love." Maipaa responded gracefully.

White Bear barked. She always knew what was going on. "Let's go, White Bear." I gently commanded her, as was my manner.

As we reached the bottom of the stairs, I spotted Kathleen and Shelley in the dining room having their morning coffee. I was just about to say hello when, I felt very lightheaded and seemed to become outside of myself for just a second. "What is wrong?" Maipaa asked as she held my arm.

"I'm not sure. I have never felt that way before. I'm sure it's nothing." I assured her while I was thinking just the opposite. I knew that I had just been on the edge of a void. The sun and the moon had been frozen in time for a split second and I was about to fall up into the sky. "That must have been awful good bourbon," I joked.

Kathleen and Shelley spotted us and came out to the hallway. "Are you going out to say goodbye to your brothers, Ben" Kathleen asked.

"We'll go with you," Shelley offered.

"Great," I happily responded.

As we walked out and stepped onto the street, Davy and Daniel came over to us and offered their goodbyes and good luck wishes. "Ben, when you get to Colorado City, tell those boys from the Pinkerton Agency that I will meet them at Devil's Head Mountain in two day's time," Daniel informed me.

Davy then remarked, "I'll be back here with them settlers at about sunset tomorrow, Ben."

"Okay brothers, take care of your safety, and I'll see you soon," I pleaded.

Behind Debra the doors opened, and Doc and Wyatt came out of the saloon. "We have had our morning whiskey, boys. We are ready to ride now," Doc said with satisfaction.

"Yes. Let's go get them ruffians now, Daniel," Wyatt said with a smile.

As everyone rode out their separate ways, I couldn't help but feel very proud to have a family such as I had. Maipaa, White Bear and I made our way over to Little Scott's to borrow a wagon for our trip to Colorado City and bid our goodbye to Shelley and Kathleen on the way back out of town. Kathleen yelled out, "Ben, you need to get back here soon and safe. You'll have plenty of Mayor's business to take care of when you get back."

"I'll want you to come to the school and give a speech to the kids also, Ben," Shelley demanded.

"Okay, you can count on me." I smiled and commanded our two chestnut horses to move to begin our journey to Colorado City.

CHAPTER FIVE

That morning reflected the best of beauty in Colorado in any decade or century. The bright yellow aspens glistened in the morning eastern sun. The wildlife came alive as if in a slide show. Brightly colored clouds hovered over us like a blanket of comfort. The sound of the rushing water proclaimed its freedom from the snow packed mountain in a brave way. The horses took delight in the pleasure of a slow descent. Maipaa and I delighted in the freedom of life. That trip was the glory of life to remember forever. But, I knew in the back of my time-traveling mind that it was only the calm before the storm. I knew that I had found myself only to be lost again. Nonetheless, it was a moment anyone would live a lifetime for the joy of.

Then a moment later, the whisper of a glorious morning turned into the shout of sudden fear. White Bear stopped in her tracks. Her ears perked up into the air and her nose sniffed in a hurry. She looked to the west in alert. The horses began to balk and tremble. Then a loud roar came from the gulley to our side, and a mule deer flashed by with all out speed in front of us. We could then see the unbelievable horror of a beast, the likes of which is only talked about in generations from the unknown. It ran after the deer just as quickly as it could. It was a dark, tall and hairy creature with large eyes of destructive intent. It looked at us quickly without stopping and gave us an intimidating growl. It had the appearance of a grizzly bear but ran upright. We only saw it for a few seconds and then could hear it in its menacing chase for just a few more moments, then silence again. Maipaa held onto me tight and whispered the word, "Hatapi."

White Bear quickly moved between the Hatapi and our wagon to protect us. She was big and could be menacing when provoked as well, but I called to her, "It's okay White Bear, It's okay." I did not want her to mix it up with that thing. I drew my two Colt revolvers and handed the reins to Maipaa. "Lead us forward and fast!"

"Yes, Ben," she calmly responded and coaxed the nervous horses to go. Did they ever get going; they ran like the wind. We were out of sight of that creature quickly with White Bear running behind and guarding our rear.

As we neared noon and were far away from that startle, I said to Maipaa, "I think we are in the clear now. I remember a stage coach stop just to the east. The South Platte River is on the plains right next to the ranch built there by a good friend, Bret and his wife Bonnie. They live there with Bonnie's mom, also named Bonnie, and their wise young daughter Sarina Claire. In fact her name is symbolic of peace and wisdom. We'll take that left fork and be there very soon. We can rest the horses, and we might be lucky if Bonnie G and her mom Bonnie are cooking lunch for the stage. I have stopped there many times on my journeys to Colorado Springs. They have become very good friends of mine and I enjoy their company.. Sarina has surely got the makings of a school teacher. I hope to help build a school house nearby someday. Bret came down to Colorado from Dakota Territory with his brothers to build homes for the miners. He met Bonnie G while building a saloon for her in the Woodlands Park and married her quickly. They built their ranch in the perfect place for the overland stage to offer them a nice sum to outfit their coaches on a regular basis. There it is, see the corrals behind those aspen trees. Let's get on over there. I am sure we are out of danger now, and we can rest."

As we pulled up next to the corral, Sarina came running out of the house yelling, "Uncle Ben, where have you been! We missed you. I will go tell everyone you are here!"

Bonnie G came out quickly with her mom Bonnie and that wide-eyed smile of hers. "Hi Ben! You have managed to get here once again just in time to eat. You must be missing my homemade jelly." She quipped.

"I miss it every day, Bonnie G, and your fine company too. This is Maipaa; she will be my wife soon," I beamed with satisfaction.

"I bet you miss our cooking too," Mom Bonnie said.

"Well congratulations, Ben and Maipaa." Surprised, Bonnie G walked over to greet Maipaa with a hand shake.

"What did I just hear?" Bret asked with just as much surprise as he walked out of the barn.

"You sure did hear right." I responded as I got down from the wagon gently and with a slow limp.

"What happened to your foot, Uncle Ben?" Sarina asked.

"I was shot by a crazy man. Don't worry though, Doc Holiday took the bullet out, and it will be okay," I told her.

"Is that why you wear guns now, Uncle Ben?" Sarina asked.

"No, I have those because I am the Mayor of Forest City now," I responded.

"Well, you sure are moving up in the world, Ben!" Bret smirked with that Minnesota grin.

"Yes, a great job and a beautiful wife, all in the same day." I gloated like a big shot.

"You should let us have the wedding here for you, Ben." Bonnie G offered.

"That would be perfect," I complied, and Maipaa nodded with happiness.

"Great. I'll build a gazebo for the ceremony," added Bret anxiously.

"Okay, but we have to wait for my brothers to set the date."

"Let's get out of the hot sun, and I'll put food out on the table for us all," Mom Bonnie offered.

As we sat down for a terrific meal, I began to tell them about the Hatapi. Bonnie G, Bonnie and Sarina gasped in fright, while Bret didn't seem surprised. Maipaa was wise enough to calm them though. She said, "Do not worry, he only tries to protect the berry patches in the gully from deer and other animals that would eat the berries. That is what they eat. My tribe has lived in peace with them for generations. I have seen one of them up close when I was young, and it meant no harm to me. You should not fear them as long as you leave their food alone."

"I have seen this creature too," Bret announced. "I was cutting wood for the corral and noticed him watching me. I think he was just curious though. After a while he just walked away slowly. I will say that the horses are spooked by him occasionally. I think he is a friend though and keeps the bears and mountain lions away," he said and then changed the subject and asked, "Ben, where are you off too if you are not selling whiskey any longer?"

I then began to tell them all about the goings on in Forest City the day before and about the murderous bad guys. "I'm going to Colorado City to get help for my brother Daniel from the Pinkerton Agency. We hope to get there by sunset and stay over at the Antlers' Hotel," I said.

"Well then, I will go out and tend to your horses and bring some food for White Bear," Bret offered as he got up quickly.

"Thanks Bret. I'll give you a hand." I was relieved to have such good friends.

"I will help clean up," Maipaa said as she followed Bonnie and Mom to the kitchen.

As we got ready to leave, Bonnie G asked us to give them the date for the wedding as soon as it was set, and they would make preparations. Bret brought a shotgun out of the barn and said, "Just in case, Ben."

"Okay, thanks, you take care too." I shook his hand and then asked White Bear to get the horses moving. She complied and we were off.

CHAPTER SIX

We arrived in Colorado City just in time to see the purple clouds disappear behind Pikes Peak. The streets were alive with people coming and going. I steered the wagon directly to the *Sun* newspaper office and asked a young cowboy sitting on the porch for directions to the Pinkerton Agency. "What do you want with them?" he sneered sarcastically.

"I want to deliver a request to the boss man," I shot back. "What is your name?" I asked with curiosity.

"Harry Longabaugh." The young man sheepishly answered. "Do you know where there might be some work for me and my cousin?" He asked as he pointed to another young man standing on the porch. "His name is John Gulden. We have just arrived from Pennsylvania in search of a living."

"I am the mayor of Forest City," I replied. "We will be going back there first thing in the morning. Forest City is a growing town and I am sure there will be work there for spirited young fellows like you two. If you would like to ride along with us, I will try to help you get work there," I informed them.

John quickly said, "Sounds okay to me, Harry."

"Yep, sounds good to me too." Harry replied.

"We will meet you here at sun up. Now, how do I get to the Pinkerton agency?" I asked.

"It is just up those stairs." Harry pointed across the street.

"Great, will you take our wagon and horses to the stable for two bits?" I asked.

"I will be happy to sir." John took the reins and we went across the street to get that help for Daniel.

As we walked into the office, three brawny men sitting around the table having a serious discussion stopped their conversation and looked in our direction. I handled the introductions. "I am Ben Silver. This is Maipaa and our faithful dog, White Bear. My brother Daniel has asked me to come here and request your assistance in the capture of three murderous men up in the vicinity of Phantom Trail." I pleaded. "Daniel has asked me to tell you to meet him at Devil's Head Mountain in two days time."

The tallest man stood up and said, "I am Matt Baker. These two fellows are Steve and Nate. They work for me in this territory. I am afraid I have some bad news for you, Ben." Matt's grave tone made me nervous. "I have just received a telegraph from Wyatt Earp in Leadville. He said that your brother set off from them to follow a separate trail of riders, and they heard gun shots after a while. They raced to the spot of the shots, but could only find Daniel's horse. They looked all afternoon, before going to Leadville to send a telegraph for our assistance with all speed."

My heart fell to the floor. I was shaken. "Daniel is too clever to be taken by those bad guys. What could have happened to him?" I then became speechless and worried. The light headed feeling came back to me again. I felt like I was dying.

"Sit down Ben," Maipaa demanded. "You do not look good."

White Bear sensed my ill feeling and began to whimper. Matt immediately grabbed his guns and said to me, "We are leaving immediately and will ride all night to help locate your brother on first light. Steve and Nate, let's go!" The other two men were already on their feet "Ben, we will find Daniel. Don't you worry." Matt's reassurance as they began to leave encouraged me.

"I will find my brother Davy and follow you. Thanks for your help."

"Daniel is our brother too." Nate put his hand on my shoulder as his words touched my ears. Then they ran out the door in a hell of a hurry.

As I sat in the chair, White Bear came over and sat right next to me, looking up in wonderment. I became more and more weary. My light headedness turned into a feeling of flight. Maipaa became a vision fading into the past. Then the darkness and time traded positions. That's all that I remember from that time. In a moment I was back at Kathleen's boarding house and I was Charlie again. Sarah was sitting right next to me. Everything was quiet in the old town. Only the life's memory of a time long ago was left for me and Sarah. All I had left was the register from behind Kathleen's counter, my dog Sarah and a whistle of wind blowing through a broken window. I didn't think it was possible to feel so empty with the full life I had been leading. But this was worse, much worse. My brother had disappeared. I sat there on the floor as long as I could. I was trying to concentrate myself back to the past again. With total exhaustion, I realized that the feat of time travel could only be accomplished by another freak moment of nature, and I would not know if this could ever happen again. I walked dejectedly out the door and back to the Jeep with Sarah. How could I ever know what had happened to my brother Daniel? I didn't get a chance to alert Davy. What about Maipaa? I had left her alone in that office. Now, I had to wonder if this was just another dream. I reached weakly into my pocket for the car keys. That's when I thought about the 1886 penny. I had picked it up from the dirt streets. I went directly to the horse post and there it was, albeit rusted, but there. It wasn't a dream; it was real. The penny proved it, and I left it there for good luck. I was filled with adrenaline and joy. Maybe I could find a way back again. "I am too stubborn to quit," I thought. Then I got Sarah in the Jeep and drove home as quickly as I could to report this unbelievable event to Meredith. I knew that she would have a rational explanation. On the way, I put my mind to work trying to figure out a way back.

While I was thinking about the conditions in which this miracle had happened, my memory shook out a tidbit of history from my previous research. I had remembered the name of Tesla. Nicola was his first name. He had been called a man out of time. His research had more to do with electricity than it did with time. But I had a crazy thought to see how he created electricity to see if I could duplicate the circumstances under which I was transported in time. As crazy a thought that was, I was beginning to grab hold of the stubborn determination I carried in my guts when I really wanted something. I could only remember that Tesla was said to have created devices which harnessed alternating electrical current. I was beginning to create a plan. The very next day I would be at the library and Pioneer's Museum where I could get more information on Tesla's inventions. Meredith was bound to think I've lost it for sure now. "Oh well, she has probably been thinking that for a long time now." I chuckled at myself once again.

As I passed a town called Bust, Colorado-Population 2-I suddenly realized that I might be able to find out what happened to my brother while doing my history research. I had been successful before in finding Christiana's Secret with my stubborn research tactics. After all, people like Doc Holiday, Wyatt Earp, Harry Longabaugh-The Sundance Kid-and Leroy Parker-Butch Cassidy were famous enough to have lots of articles about their lives. I didn't know about the Silver Brothers but I knew where to go to find out. That thought relaxed me a little until Sarah and I passed a tourist attraction near Old Colorado City called Ghost Town. That gave me an eerie and chilled disposition and a very empty feeling. I had always been all about family, and I couldn't rest until I found out what happened to Daniel Silver. He was so much like my current life's brother, Donnie. He had recently died at a young age, and now I had lost that beloved one twice in two lifetimes. Still though, he was always with me, and so was Dad.

CHAPTER SEVEN

Meredith had just walked out the front door when we pulled up out front of the house. "Charlie, why are you home so early?" She asked in surprise. That is when I immediately recognized that she must have been Maipaa. She surely was the same spirit. That is why I fell in love with her so quickly in this life. Wow!

"You might want to go back in the house with me and sit down for a while. This is going to take a while." I chuckled and she rolled her eyes. As I recalled everything that I thought had happened, I began to notice that 'I knew it' look on Mer's face.

"I was wondering," she said with certainty. "I had a dream while taking a nap this morning, Charlie. I don't know where we were, but I remember part of what you have been telling me of what happened. Then, I remember waking up and being traumatized. You had suddenly disappeared. I remember that my name was Maipaa. We were about to be married and then you disappeared. How could we both have had the same dream? I must have been pulled back into our forgotten reality. It really isn't that far fetched when I think about it. When we first met in 1979, I knew for an instant that we had been together before. When I first saw this house, I heard Christiana call out to me from across the street, and I knew that this life of ours was a scheduled stop on our yellow brick road. Can you do some of your research magic, Charlie? Can you find out what happened to us and your brother? Can you find that treasure on Phantom Trail? Why don't you bring White Bear, oh, I mean Sarah back up there and see what you can find out."

"You were there!" I shouted. "You knew Sarah's name. She was there with us. I sure will go back and I'll also get back to my favorite research places. I am going to start with research about Nicola Tesla to see if I can duplicate the atmospheric anomaly to return in time."

"Do you think that you can really do that, Charlie?" she quizzed me.

"Well, sure Mer. We know it can happen. We just have to figure out how. I'll start today," I assured her.

"Charlie, there is one more thing. In my dream I remember our good friends Bret and Bonnie and their mom Bonnie, and daughter Sarina. Were they there?"

"Yes Mer, they sure were. Wow!"

"Oh Charlie, I almost forgot. You got a phone call this morning from someone in New York. His name is Bruce Jenkins. He said that he and his wife, Jeannie, had met you at the library in Glens Falls. They are doing some research on the early life of Bat Masterson and hoped that you might be able to help them since he spent time in Colorado," Mer recounted.

"Oh sure, I remember them. They are psychic researchers. They have an uncanny ability to replay some pieces of history in their subconscious. I'll be glad to call and tell them what I know. I'll call now. Do you have the phone number?" I asked.

"Here it is Charlie." Mer handed me the note.

I paced toward the phone in the kitchen and nimbly dialed the numbers. "Hello Bruce, this is Charlie. It is good to hear from you. Meredith told me that you are researching Bat Masterson."

"Yes Charlie, thanks for calling back. Jeannie and I have had some unsettling subconscious thought about Bat Masterson. Something very violent must have happened around him. We keep seeing a shooting and then death." Bruce's voice trailed off with despair.

"I do recall some particulars about him, Bruce. He was a buffalo hunter, army scout, lawman, US Marshal and also a sports editor in New York before he died at his desk in 1921. I have a quote written by him just before his death and found on his typewriter. It reads, 'There are those who argue that everything breaks even in this old dump of a world of ours. I suppose these ginks who argue that way hold that because the rich man gets ice in the summer and the poor man gets ice in the winter things are breaking even for both. Maybe so, but I'll swear I can't see it that way.' I also remember that he was a Deputy for Wyatt Earp in Dodge City and a Marshal here in Trinidad, Colorado."

"That is useful info Charlie, but there must be something else. Jeannie is on the other extension. She has a question for you."

"Hi Charlie, it is great to talk with you again. That is great info on Bat, but there must be something else. I keep seeing violence, and it ends with Bat shooting two men." Jeannie's voice quivered

"Well, actually Bat wasn't involved in a lot of gun fights." I said. "But, I do remember that he had two brothers. One of those brothers, whose name may have been Ed was shot by two men while he was a Marshall in Dodge City. Bat was across the street and returned fire on the two men, killing one. Does that help any?" I asked.

"That must be what we are looking for. Do you know when that may have happened?" Bruce asked.

"Not for sure Bruce, but it must have been in the late 1870's. That was before Bat went to fight on the Santa Fe side of its war with the Rio Grand Railroad. He also spent time in Tombstone before the gun fight at the OK Corral and later in Denver. That is all that I can tell you." I was sure that must be what they were looking for.

"Thank you Charlie, we owe you a favor." Jeannie sounded relieved.

"That is very good news Jeannie. Can I use it now?" I asked with a chuckle.

"Sure, Charlie, you don't waste any time. What do you need?"

"Mer and I have experienced thoughts of a previous life. My brother was lost. Can you channel in on that some time and see if you can tell me anything?" I asked, not wanting to tell them the whole story. It was, after all, a little hard to believe.

"We will call you if we get any thoughts, Charlie. Talk to you soon." Bruce thanked me and hung up the phone.

"Mer, I am going down to the Pioneer's Museum. I want to get started on my research about Nicola Tesla right away. If I am lucky, Leah or Kelly will be there to give me any hints on where to find out about his experiments with electricity and lightning," I told her with enthusiasm.

"Okay Charlie, but if you start playing with electricity, then I am going to get very nervous. Your dad always said that mechanics was not your strong suit. If you try to duplicate what he did, you could get yourself killed." A look of anguish crossed Mer's face.

"Oh honey, you know that I am way too lucky for that to happen. Just relax and let me find out what he did, and we will make a plan together before I do anything."

"Okay," Mer replied as I rushed out the door.

I arrived at the museum quickly and took the antique elevator down to the research floor where historians from all over the country came to find their historical treasures. Leah and Kelly were both there and greeted me kindly as always. "Hi Charlie, what are you researching now?" Leah asked.

"I need to know all about Nicola Tesla," I informed her.

"That is an easy one; we know all about him, Charlie," quipped Kelly.

"Yes, we sure do," Leah continued. "He was a great inventor. He created devices using electrical current that we use today. It was he who invented radio, florescent lighting and the bladeless turbine. His research paved the way to computers, robots, microwaves and space-age technologies, among other things."

"I remember reading about how Mister Tesla caused a blackout in Colorado Springs in 1899," Kelly informed me. He had been watching a thunder storm pass over from the mountains. He noticed that lightning had been forming, discharging and decreasing in regular interval. He was sure that he was seeing stationary waves."

"Yes, that is right. He was then sure that the whole planet was a conductor. That fact was what made it possible to send telegraph messages without wires and send faint modulations of the human voice. Most important to his experiments was the ability to transmit unlimited power to any point on earth without any loss." Leah said with much enthusiasm.

"He figured certain that stationary waves could be produced by using an oscillator. He said that a high ratio of transmission using electrical oscillators was definitely the most efficient way to produce those stationary waves. He perfected his equipment to produce millions of volts and very heavy currents. He and his assistant, Czito, constructed a one hundred and forty-five foot tower with a copper ball and a giant coil in the room below. Czito flipped the switch first for just one second and fire appeared at the secondary coil and electricity popped in the air above. Then Czito flipped the switch again on orders from Mister Tesla to leave it open until he gave the order to close it. Then, electricity created a great thunder of lightning above and continued until blue light filled the interior of the structure below. Lightning continued again and again until the power shut down and the whole city went dark." Kelly laughed at the thought.

"He called the electric company and found out that he had knocked out their generator and caught it on fire. They offered to take a team of repair men to fix it, but they were unwilling to serve him any more after the standby generator was installed." Leah laughed too.

"That is what I need to know," I said. "Thank both of you again for helping me."

"You can count on us anytime Charlie." Leah waved at me as I turned to leave; Kelly nodded and waved too.

As I got back into the jeep for the short ride home, I felt chilled that I could never duplicate the sort of accomplishment with lightning that Nicola had done. But I was a step further in my endeavor by having learned of this experiment. I was quite sure that the set of circumstances surrounding my transference back in time could be duplicated. What I thought I should do though was to be in that right place at the right time when Mother Nature did her thing again. Meredith was quite relieved to know that I wasn't going to be playing with electricity. "Honey, sometimes it is better to drop back and punt." My got-another-idea smile shone through.

"What are you up to now, Charlie?" Mer's crooked grin of puzzlement indicated she already knew.

"I hope to talk with as many weathermen as I can. I want to find out the specifics of the atmosphere at Forest City when my transference took place. Luck is when preparation meets opportunity, Mer. If I can make an educated guess on when to be there, maybe I can go back again and find out what happened to Daniel and us." This was my best Hail Mary pass.

"I like that idea better Charlie. That sounds a lot safer. Will you let me go with you? I want to see back too. I have a feeling that there is more to our previous lives that I want to know about," Mer pleaded.

"Sure. But we'll have to leave Mariah with your mom when we go. I don't think that is a good place for a baby." I insisted on this, as I shuddered at the thought of my sweet baby girl being around gunshots.

"I agree with you. I'll make arrangements for Mom and Dad to be on standby."

"Okay then. I'll start researching that and anything I can find in the history books about the Silver family and The Reynolds Gang on Monday." I walked over to give Sarah a treat. She had been sitting in the hallway waiting patiently for a dog bone, and I wasn't going to disappoint her.

Monday couldn't come fast enough, but when it did I went right to the local television station after work. Jack Hamilton was the meteorologist and was very eager to give me the assistance I was hoping for. "What do you need to know Charlie?"

"I want to know what conditions caused the severe thunderstorm in the region around Forest City on this past Saturday morning?"

"I can help with that." He turned his attention toward his computer. "It looks like there was a strong cold front moving southeasterly from the north. At the same time there was a warm front from the southwest with lots of moisture in the air. When they collided directly over the Mosquito mountain range, the atmosphere became very highly charged with electrical currents. Is that all you need to know?"

"Yes, thank you Jack." I was grateful for this new clue.

As I left the building, I wondered why he never asked me why I wanted to know about these things. Then I reasoned that he probably gets those sorts of questions all of the time and chalks it up to human nature. As I drove to the Penrose Library to begin my research, I wondered if I could get the weather reports for that region enough to guess when another storm would happen. But I also wondered if that door to the ghost world was still open. I was determined to find out.

I went directly to the local history section of the library. As I searched the card catalogs for the last name of Silver in the old *Gazette* newspaper, I quickly found the reference to an article about Ben Silver. The reference was to an article titled "Ben Silver named Mayor of Forest City." It gave the microfiche tape number, newspaper date, page column, and line. I immediately found the tape and loaded it onto the machine. There it was on exactly the line that was referenced on the card. The article read, "The Citizens Committee of this new mountain town called Forest City has named Ben Silver as its Mayor after he received a bullet wound courtesy of one infamous Sam Starr. Ben had been wounded in the ankle and the bullet was removed by Doc Holiday. Doc has also dispatched Same Starr with a single bullet in a shootout the next day. Mister Silver's first duty was to ride to Colorado City and meet with the Pinkerton representatives regarding a gang of murderous outlaws residing in the area of Phantom Trail." That was all that the article said. I was no further along in my investigation, but I did have confirmation of the reality of my experience, which renewed my hope.

The card catalog for newspaper articles had been divided into decades. I looked for Ben Silver in the 1890's, 1900-1910, and 1910-1920. Then I got a chilling surprise when I was looking through the 1920-1930 card Catalog in the Library. I found a card which referenced an article titled, "Colorado pioneer and longtime Mayor of Forest City dies" My heart sank as I went to the microfiche drawer to read my own obituary. I loaded the tape and went directly to the article. It was dated September 4, 1929. It read, "Ben Silver, the long time Mayor of Forest City and celebrated horse rancher died today while defending the local school children from a grizzly bear. Mister Silver gave that bear a fight he won't soon forget. Unfortunately, he succumbed to wounds suffered from the inches long claws of that viscous bear. It was said that 17 school children went on a picnic from the Shelley Dumas school house. Ben had been riding his favorite horse, Silverstar, in the area and spotted the bear stalking the children when he intervened. He was able to shoot the bear several times before running out of ammunition. He then resorted to his Bowie knife before suffering his wounds. The bear also died shortly after the fierce battle. Ben will be remembered as a local hero. He also had won the Kentucky Derby with that same horse Silverstar. He leaves a wife of 43 years, Maipaa and a daughter, Miriam, who works for a charity organization in Colorado Springs. Services and Burial will be held at his private ranch, the Golden View Ranch near Buena Vista, Colorado." I had to take a deep breath after that. But, I couldn't be more proud of who I had been. To die that way is gallant. I had a terrific wife and daughter and was a well-remembered Mayor, wow!

As I looked further into the newspaper card catalog, which was in alphabetical order. I came to a card entitled "Davy Silver honored for paving the way west." I was excited to go and get the microfiche, but I was disappointed that there was no article for Daniel. That card should have been listed before Davy's card alphabetically. I was very proud though, to read about Davy. The article read, "Davy Silver, who led many wagon trains west is being honored today at the Settlers' Museum in Boulder, Colorado. Davy settled in this Front Range city after having led over 20 groups of settlers west from St. Louis. Never a single settler had perished under his leadership. This feat was unheard of in the annals of the American west. A statue has been erected to forever stand in front of this one of a kind museum." I was glad not to read an obituary for my brother. I was very glad that he received the well deserved recognition. Going back to the card catalog I couldn't find anything whatsoever about Daniel. I was puzzled. There must have been something written about him. He was becoming famous for his captures of bad guys before he disappeared.

Before I left, I decided to look into that dastardly Reynolds gang. I started finding articles immediately. The first one was dated July 25, 1864. It read,

"Confederate rebels rob the Girard ranch in Park County. Nine bad guys get away with $3,000 and cans full of gold. They also stole $1,200 from the stage passengers. Their whereabouts are unknown."

Then, quickly I found another article dated July 26, 1964. It read, "Confederate bad guys strike again. Mr. Berry, a local man reported seeing the gang rob the McGloughlin's stage, getting $10,000. The gang also robbed rich gold miner, H.H. DeMary. Although he only carried $100, they did get his hat to boot. Mr. Berry reports that the gang was last seen at the Michigan Stage Stop near Jefferson. Mr. Berry plans to warn settlers." Those guys were really raising hell, I thought. The next article was dated two days later. It read, "Confederate gang still raiding in the Platte Canyon. Many robberies reported. A posse is being dispatched from Denver to round up the dastardly Bandits." The library was closing, so I left the research for another day and went home, encouraged by finding some of the history but downtrodden by not finding information on Daniel.

CHAPTER EIGHT

"What is the matter, Charlie?" Mer asked as I walked in the door. "You look depressed."

"I'm only half depressed, honey," I replied dejectedly.

"How could that be?" Her puzzled look met my eyes.

"Well, I found my fate and that of Davy's, but there was no article about Daniel."

"Don't worry Charlie. I've known you too long and know you are too stubborn to not find out all there is to know." She beamed with pride at this statement.

Then I perked up and said, "You're right. I sure will find out, no matter what." Her statement of confidence seemed to be all I needed to get my positive drive back.

As we walked up the stairs for the night, a loud thunder cracked from the sky. I had a vision of an Apache Indian and an Army General. "I just had a vision of Geronimo. I think that I also saw General Miles."

"Are you sure? How do you know it was those two people specifically?" Mer cocked her head to the side, and that look matched her, what's-going-on-now tone.

"I read about them in my research a few years ago. I saw their photos in a book about the Army's battle with Geronimo in the Southwest. But, that was in

Arizona. I don't know what they would have to do with Colorado. But the time frame was 1886." These puzzles were starting to overwhelm me.

"Charlie, I think you are just overly tired. Let's go to bed and get some rest," Mer sighed.

I awoke, in a startle. "Mer, wake up. I know why I had a vision of Geronimo and General Miles. I was in Skeleton Canyon in September of 1886. It was just a coincidence that Geronimo was surrendering to General Miles at that very moment."

"Well, thanks for waking me up to tell me such important news, Charlie," She grunted. Awake now but none too happy about it, she asked, "What were you doing in that place?"

"You should have asked what we were doing there," I giggled. "You—Maipaa—and I were going to Mexico for our honeymoon!" My excitement at the connections had me wide awake.

"That's nice Charlie. Now, can we get back to sleep? Mer grumbled and turned over. She was not nearly as excited.

"But, you don't understand the importance of that!"

"Okay Charlie. I'm listening." Mer turned back over and glared at me through half-open eyes.

"That could only mean that the mystery of my lost brother had been solved. I would not have stopped looking for him until we found him." I was relieved at this new revelation.

"Well that is great Charlie. I hope it was good news." Mer whispered that last part before closing her eyes.

"I wish I knew, Mer. I sure do wish I knew," I whispered back and went to sleep.

I rested for the next few days and when I awoke Saturday the telephone was ringing. Mer came up the stairs and said, "Are you awake, Charlie? Jeanie, from New York is on the phone and wants to talk to you."

"Sure honey, I'll get up." I anxiously hopped out of bed.

"Hello Jeanie. How have you been doing?"

"I am fine Charlie. But, Bruce and I have been having some thoughts that are quite disturbing. We are seeing you in a mountain gulch. You are in danger. We see a man hidden in the rocks behind you with a gun pointed at you. He is a bad man Charlie. We can both see him with a snarl on his face, and he means to kill you for sure! You must be careful. Are you going up in the mountains any time soon?" Her hurried words couldn't hide a caring tone.

"Yes, I was thinking about going today. I need to see if I can go back in time again to find out what happened to my brother Daniel." I explained all of what I had been through in my return to Forest City.

"Well Charlie, I wasn't sure but we have known some of what happened to you already. We have been seeing it since we talked with you on the phone. It is going to happen again Charlie. You are going to go back in time again with Sarah and this time Meredith will be there!"

"Oh, that is great news. I have been trying to figure out how to make that happen."

"You can't make that happen on your own will, Charlie. There are forces at work that you don't know about. They are powerful forces that control the twists and turns of time. You have a connection to the spirit world which has given you a key to that door. But, you can not use that key even if you knew how to. There is a friendly spirit on your shoulder who turns the key for you. It is a spiritual key. We think that this spirit is a woman who has had a deep and grateful relationship with you. We can't see her. We can only see a good light. She had very strong energy, and she wants to protect you. But, there is one thing that you should know Charlie. When we have the vision of a bad guy wanting to shoot you, we can't see her near you. I wish we could be there to help you." Jeanie pleaded with sincerity for me to be careful.

"I think I know who the spirit is. Her name is Christiana Fitsimmonds." I then informed her all about finding her diary in Dead Man's Gulch and then researching her history to find out that she had been my Great, Great Grandmother.

"We had thought that her name might have started with an M though, Charlie," Jeanie replied.

"She was given the name of Mamaci Paa by the Ute Indians. They found her hiding behind a waterfall after killing her brother and other companions in the gulch. They adopted her, and the Chief's son married her. Her family never knew what happened to her. If you want to come and visit, then I will have time to tell you all about Christiana's Secret and the lost treasure of Dead Man's Gulch."

"Oh yes, we would love to go out to Colorado to visit you. Can we come out there for a three-day weekend next week?"

"Sure, that would be good. I would like for you and Bruce to go to Forest City with Mer and me and Sarah. Let me know when your plane lands and I will pick you up at the airport. We have a big house and an extra bedroom. If you can get reservations for Friday, then we can go on Saturday to the mountains." My anticipation of the outing had my nearly jumping.

"Okay Charlie. But would you be careful if you go up there today?" .

"Christiana will watch over me," I said with a grin toward Mer.

After I hung up the phone, Mer said, "Charlie, are you going up there today? I wanted to go with you, but I promised to go shopping with Mom and Mariah today."

"That is okay honey, you go shopping. I am going to take Sarah up and just look around some more. I don't think anything will happen today. You can come along next week with Jeanie and Bruce," I said calmly.

"Sure Charlie, that is fine. But, you always tell me that nothing will happen and something always does," Mer said and shook her head. "What about the bad guy Jeanie mentioned?" She had been listening to my phone conversation with Jeanie on the extension.

"If that were to happen, I am sure that Sarah will warn me," I said with confidence.

"Charlie, I'd feel better if you would ask Uncle Johnny to go with you, I talked with him a few days ago and I'm sure he will be at Flo's Restaurant." Mer's eyes told me I better call Uncle Johnny.

"That's a great idea! I'll give him a call." I picked up the phone right away to call Uncle Johnny and started laughing out loud. If you knew him, you would know why. He is absolutely the funniest man I ever knew and the bravest too. He saved my life from a grizzly bear in Dead Man's Gulch. It was easy to ask him to come along. He said yes to the trip before I gave him all of the details. We decided to drive through the Platte Canyon on the way up to Forest City to have a look around. I planned to do more research about the Reynolds Gang. I thought it would be helpful to look at the lay of the land to have a clear picture of the area. We made arrangements to leave early. I packed sandwiches and beer as always, and of course, treats for Sarah.

Mer woke Sarah and me early that morning. I called Uncle Johnny an hour before I was to pick him up, as is standard procedure. Sarah greeted him with a kiss when we picked him up at Flo's restaurant in Park County. Dogs know things, don't they? I decided to take highway 285 through the Platte canyon. That is a safer route in the mountains when the dark is all about. There is much wildlife crossing those mountain roads. An elk or bear can do much damage to a vehicle, as can a mule deer. By the time we got to a small town named Bailey, near the South Platte River, the sun was up, and the view was tremendous! The Kenosha mountain range's awesome beauty glimmered in the light, reminding us how it is rich with gold. The road we traveled was paved over the previous stage coach road to Denver. We took a break at the entrance to Geneva Gulch. Little did we know at that time, that this was the focus place for many treasure hunters who have been looking for the Reynolds Gang treasure which is said to be buried here.

When Sarah decided that it was time to go again, she put her big paw up on my lap and barked gently. We laughed and started driving into the gulch. After a half mile, the gulch opened up into a huge canyon with steep rock peaks on both sides. A swampy area was on the left, and a small creek crossed the dirt road leading from a pool that caught the high mountain melt. We talked about how difficult it must have been to travel that mountain range on horses. Uncle Johnny thought it would be a good idea to sample the stream for gold dust. "Watch out for bears though, Charlie" He chuckled and playfully punched my arm.

I agreed and walked around back of the jeep for the gold pan that we always carried with us. We looked closely in the stream for black sand, which always accompanies gold. We spotted a pocket quickly behind a boulder in the stream and started panning. There certainly was a few tiny flowers of gold, but it didn't seem enough to work all day at and have it pay. We decided to move on up to Forest city and find our millions another day. On the way over the Kenosha Pass we passed Hall's Valley. I had an eerie feeling as I looked to the right, down the gulch. The road narrowed into a small cut in the canyon walls. I noticed something though that gave me pause for thought. A small creek flowed from that canyon under the road we traveled. It emptied into the north branch of the north fork of the South Platte River. It is well known to many in this region that the South Platte is a fruitful place for gold panning. My first thought was that that creek must carry the free gold from the Kenosha Mountains into the South Platte. As we drove further I thought about Dead Man's Gulch a short distance from where we were. Uncle Johnny must have been thinking the same thing because we both smiled at the same moment.

That is the moment all hell broke loose. Elk were all around us! I hit the brakes fast: the jeep swerved back and forth. Sarah came in to the front seat with us. I just missed one elk, then another. We were in a gully before I knew it. Dust permeated the air. I couldn't see. I could hear the bellows of the fleeing elk herd. Sarah whimpered, and Uncle Johnny said, "Wow, that was damn good driving Charlie."

I replied, "Just a little of that famous luck of mine I guess."

We got out of the Jeep to survey the damage. We hadn't hit a single elk, but the jeep was in the ditch at a steep angle, barely upright. We didn't dare go forward a single inch. Uncle Johnny quickly grabbed the rope from our kit in the back of the Jeep. He then said, "C'mon Sarah." Before I knew what he was up to, he tied the rope to the front left bumper and then darted across the road and wrapped it twice around a tree and then to Sarah. He grabbed the rope too and said, "Hit it, Charlie." I pressed the gas pedal as he and Sarah tugged on the rope. Just like that, we were free and on our way.

"Just a minor inconvenience for us guys." Uncle Johnny said with a big ha, ha. Then he grabbed the hotel register I had put in the back seat from the boarding house. He rustled around with the back cover and said, "There's something else in here Charlie."

"What do you mean?" I hadn't noticed anything else, so I was a bit confused.

Uncle Johnny pulled out three sheets of old paper from inside. "This is what I mean."

I pulled over immediately as he began to read:

It is not riches that I want
I witnessed a burial
Of men it was not
When I was small
With my dad was I
When a calling from nature
Caused me to take refuge under a tree
It was not far from here
On vacation were we
I saw two men I did fear
With rocks and cloth and cans heavy
They then buried their secret
This from my lips did no man ever hear

-Kathleen Melanson

"It's a secret poem!" I whistled. "What is on the other two pages?"

"I'm not sure Charlie. I can't read them. The writing is too faded." Uncle Johnny looked disgusted as he studied the pages. Taking the papers, from him, I couldn't read them either.

"Must be that Reynolds gang treasure, Uncle Johnny," I said.

"Sure is Charlie; she must have hidden that secret all of her life." Uncle Johnny nodded in confirmation.

"Maybe we can figure out how to read the rest." Even I wasn't sure how.

"Okay Charlie, let's go see where you have been. I want to see this Ghost Town of yours!" Uncle Johnny sounded content to move on.

As we drove by the old buildings, not a sound could be heard; we were quiet with wonder. We got out and walked through the buildings as I told Uncle Johnny my story. He didn't say anything, just tried to make sense of it. As I sat down in the old saloon, I heard a rattling noise. "Don't move Charlie!" Uncle Johnny screamed. He picked up an old bar stool, broke off the leg, and threw it behind me quick as the eye could see. The rattling stopped; I looked around and there, right behind me, was a dead rattle snake.

"Nice shot, Uncle John. I guess Mer was right about bringing you along." I smiled and breathed deeply.

"Yah Charlie, I can't take you anywhere," he laughed as he walked out of the saloon: I followed, laughing just as hard. We were on our way home with another great memory.

CHAPTER NINE

The next day I awoke to a surprise visit from my brother Roger, his wife Carol and my fun sister Kathy. Sarah barked as a motor home pulled up out front of the house. Three smiling faces came walking up the front porch. "Did we surprise you Charlie?" Kathy asked with a chuckle.

"You sure did." I replied. "Are you guy's crazy? Did you just jump into the motor home and drive 2,000 miles on the spur of the moment?"

"We must be crazy. We're having a great time though." Roger said with a grin.

"What are we having for breakfast Charlie?" Carol asked.

"Anything my favorite sister in law wants." I said.

Mer headed toward the kitchen saying, "Is everyone hungry for my famous sausage gravy?" Sarah barked. She knew those words. We all laughed and followed Mer to the kitchen for coffee and breakfast.

Roger looked over at me and said. "Well, it's like this Charlie. We were all sitting in the back yard and talking about our gold panning trips in Colorado. Carol and Kathy insisted that I take some time off of work and take them out here for a couple of days to see if we could get you to take us to find some more gold."

"I am always willing to do that." I assured him with a big smile. "How long can you stay?" I asked.

"We have to leave tomorrow night." Roger told me. "I have to be back to work on Thursday."

"Okay, then we can go up to our favorite gulch where we found gold the last time you were here. If you want to take your motor home, we can spend the night and be back tomorrow afternoon." I suggested.

"I hope you didn't tell anyone else about our secret place Charlie." Kathy said with that sister kind of look in her eye.

"You'll find out when we get you another one of those big nuggets." I replied with that teasing brother look on my face.

Carol laughed and said, "I want one too, Charlie! Any size nugget would be fine with me."

"Well, I had better find more than one nugget to pay for all that gas on this trip." Roger informed me as we all laughed without feeling any pressure.

After breakfast we got ready to go and I noticed Sarah sitting in front of the door. She always knew when I was getting ready to go somewhere. "Do you have room for Sarah?" I asked Roger.

"Sure. We can't leave her home. We might need her protection today if we run into any of those wild critters you are famous for finding." Roger replied with a very serious tone.

"Okay Sarah, lets go for a ride." I said as she pounced up and down with excitement. We all piled into the motor home with smiles and anticipation of our new adventure. The trip up Ute Pass was hilarious. Kathy was cracking jokes without end and the mood for all was joyful. Bright skies and a gliding eagle led the way through the city above the clouds as we passed Woodland Park and into the unpopulated mountain terrain. As I gave directions to Roger, he asked, "Are you sure this is the right way? It doesn't look familiar to me."

I calmly reassured him that I was taking him on a new shortcut that I had found. "The scenery is better this way." I told him.

Carol quickly quipped, "You better not get us lost Charlie. We only have two days." Everyone laughed. That is about the time that I asked Roger to turn left on an unmarked dirt road. He seemed worried, but had confidence in me. The squirrels ran left and right. A pair of humming birds whizzed by the motor home as if to say get out of my way. The clouds gathered as if to give a warning. The air became scarce of oxygen and something seemed wrong. Just then, the motor home stalled. Everyone suddenly had a scared look on their face. Carol screamed at Roger, "What is wrong Rog?"

Kathy said quickly, "The engine stopped running." Mer had a look of surprise on her face. I was concerned until I looked over at Roger. He had a serious face on, but I knew that he had an ace up his sleeve. "Well, the battery is dead guys. I guess we'll have to walk now."

"The alternator is dead, isn't it Rog?" I asked

"Yep, sure is, we aren't going anywhere now." Roger grinned while he couldn't hold back his secret.

"You have a backup alternator somewhere, don't you?" I asked with a grin.

"Yep, thought this might happen." he said. First Kathy laughed, and then everyone followed. Who else but Roger would keep a backup alternator in their vehicle?

"That's great Rog, but what about the dead battery?" I asked him.

"I've got that covered too." he responded with confidence. "This motor home has 3 batteries in it. The engine has 1 battery and there are 2 more fore the home." He chuckled.

"How long will that take Roger?" Mer asked with concern.

"It'll take about a half hour. Why are you worried about that? We have all day." Roger answered.

"Well, I don't want to make everyone nervous, but those clouds are looking very ominous." Mer said with that 'oh no' look on her face.

Kathy looked over at her and asked, "Why are you worried about that? We are in this big motor home."

"I am a little worried because we have flash floods in Colorado and we are in a valley with that stream over there going through it." Mer said while pointing at a little stream close by.

"Can you hurry up Rog?" Carol blurted out quickly.

"Yes, please do." Kathy added. "I don't think this motor home converts into a boat."

"I'm on it right now. Can you give me a hand Charlie?" Roger said quickly. We jumped out and started working as quickly as we could. That was exactly the moment the thunder crackled and the water came out of the sky like I had never seen in all of the years that I had lived in Colorado. Roger and I were soaked but continued to work. I glanced quickly through the windshield and noticed the concerned look on the girls faces. Then I turned to survey the terrain as Roger was putting on the last bolts. I noticed a clearing in the Aspen trees going slightly up the side of a hill.

"Can you get the motor home up through those trees?" I asked Roger.

"Just barely Charlie, it will be close." he said with a question mark.

"We had better hurry. That stream is now a river and it is rising quickly. We only have minutes before we are in big trouble." I said with much worry.

"Hurry guys, hurry, the water is getting higher very fast!" Carol yelled out. Roger quickly connected one of the house batteries and we jumped in soaking wet. Roger turned the ignition key and nothing happened. Silence permeated the air.

"Oh, I forgot to connect the ground wire." Roger said to everyone's relief. He jumped out and got it connected. When he turned the key again the engine started like magic.

"Now, what are we going to do?" Kathy asked. "The water is up to the wheels."

"We are going up that hill, through the trees." Roger said as he put the gear shift in low and started up the hill. We were getting away from the quickly rising water. None of us knew if we could get high enough to escape the flash flood. I was very scared. Sarah barked as a herd of elk quickly ran past us up the hill.

"At least we are going the right way." Mer said. "Those elk know where to go."

"Yah, but we can't go where they are going." Roger said as he slowly squeezed the motor home through the trees with just inches to spare. The rain was coming down so hard that it sounded like we were inside of a metal drum. Actually, we were.

"I can't go any higher. Those trees are too close together." Roger told us.

"All we can do now is wait and hope." I said with no other words or thoughts. We had gotten to that spot with no time to spare. The flash flood came crashing down the valley. It rocked the motor home back and forth as it hit us. We all gasped in fright. The rocking continued but the motor home was holding its ground.

"We drove 2,000 miles for this?" Kathy exclaimed in an effort to release the stress with some humor like she always did. We all laughed as we sensed that we were going to survive. The water level dropped quickly as if it were a monster sensing defeat with its prey. As we watched the monster going away, Mer asked for a glass of wine. She had never been the first to ask for a drink, but she was this day. We all were thirsty and got a drink while we thought about our mortality.

"Let's get out of here right now." Kathy insisted.

"We might get stuck in the mud." I informed her.

"The sun will return soon and the ground will dry." Mer assured her.

As I looked down at the stream, I had a thought and said out loud. "You know what I am thinking."

"Do we really want to know Charlie?" Kathy quipped. "Does it involve any lions, and tigers, and bears, or flash floods?"

With a chuckle and a smile I responded. "No, but it does involve gold."

"Oh, well you have my ear Charlie." Carol quickly said.

"We are at the base of the Kenosha Mountains. That stream over there comes from the top of these mountains. There is gold in those mountains. That flash flood may have brought some of that gold down to us." I informed them.

"Now, you are talking Charlie." Kathy said with great interest.

"We can camp right here for the night and let the road dry out." Roger told us. "I just need to level the motor home right here. Can you give me a hand Charlie?"

As I jumped out of the motor home I heard Mer say, "Oh look, there is a baby elk over there. It looks like it is hurt. I have to help it." She then ran down the hill. "Charlie, come here. We have to carry it back up there and protect it until its mom comes back." When I got closer, I could see that soaking wet little critter was scared to death.

"Wait. Here is a blanket for it." Carol said on the run down the hill." Then, Roger and Kathy followed. We all placed the little guy in the blanket and carried it back up the hill while it whimpered. As I looked back, I could see that we were just in time. A mountain lion was sneaking away. He had been poised for dinner. Mer found an extra baby bottle in her purse and filled it with milk. She fed the little guy and he quickly stopped his whimpering. I have always thought that if I get reincarnated, I want to be one of Mer's pets. The baby elk was barely finished with the milk when its mom appeared. She was peeking around a tree wondering what to do. We moved the baby a little closer to her and walked away. The baby immediately jumped up and ran to her. They walked away as the mom turned and looked at us as if to say thank you.

While Roger and I were leveling the motor home, I whispered to him, "Did you see that mountain lion?"

"I sure did. That was a close one. I didn't say anything because I didn't want to scare the girls." Roger said with a sigh. "Do you really think we have a chance of finding some gold here?" she asked me.

"I have read that some geologists think that less than half of the gold in Colorado has been found." I said. "I know that gold comes down the South Platte River and the Arkansas River. These mountains are between the two rivers. Dead Man's gulch is on the other side of this mountain. I am pretty sure that the stream down there is actually the North Branch of the South Fork of the South Platte River. I am pretty sure that gold is traveling down that stream from somewhere in that mountain." I said while pointing toward the top of Kenosha Pass.

"Well, that is good enough for me. Let's get the girls and have a look." Roger said with great enthusiasm and a smile. They were already on their way out of the door with their gold pans and big smiles on their faces.

"We are way ahead of you guys." Kathy said with a smirk and her most assuring confidence.

I laughed and said. "Well, lead the way little sis."

"That is exactly what I was going to do." she informed me. "Do you see that pile of rocks down there?" she asked me while pointing the way.

"I sure do. That is exactly where I would start looking. Those rocks are on the inside of the stream." I responded.

"What does that have to do with anything?" Carol asked.

"Gold is heavy. It usually falls out of the water on the inside of the river." I told her. When we get there, let's look for black sand." I requested.

"Are you kidding us? Who cares about black sand?" Kathy quizzed me.

"Black sand is heavy like gold. They hang out together like good friends." I said with confidence and a grin.

Our smiles didn't last long though. We looked through the rocks and didn't find a single nugget or any black sand. We all looked up and down the stream and came up empty handed. Dark was coming quickly now and Carol mentioned getting dinner started on the grill. That is when Roger suddenly said, "Everybody stay together and get back to the motor home quickly."

"What's wrong Rog?" I asked.

"That mountain lion is back." he said while looking in the distance. We all looked quickly and saw that devil perching for an attack. The girls all gasped at the same time and went quickly back up the hill. We all went inside and closed the door.

"What did you mean about that mountain lion being back?" Kathy asked.

"Charlie and I saw it earlier today. It was hunting the baby elk. We saw it walk away and didn't think it would come back. We didn't see any need in scaring you girls." he said.

"That thing had better not come back tomorrow." Kathy said. "I'll give him a taste of this." she said while getting a can of pepper spray out of her purse. We all laughed. Kathy is one tough cookie when she gets angry. That mountain lion would be in for big trouble if it messed around with her. It must have known that because we never saw it again.

We went to bed early but didn't get to sleep too quickly. Carol led us all in a chorus singing songs that she had thought up. The laughing is probably what really scared the mountain lion away. The next morning we were talking about our route for the trip home. We decided to go back down the mountain pass by way of a little town called Deckers. It is located on the South Fork of the South Platte River. We packed up and Roger started the engine. He put the gear in reverse and we didn't go anywhere. The rear tires were spinning in the mud. We all got out of the motor home and were wondering what to do when we saw a green Jeep coming down the dirt road. It stopped close to us and four people got out of the Jeep. They came up to talk to us. "Hello. It looks like you have a little trouble here," one of the men dressed in a uniform said.

"We are in more than a little trouble." Roger exclaimed.

"My name is Gerry." the man said. "This is Hoppy." he said while introducing the other uniformed man. "We are Wildlife officers. These two people are Ronnie and Bett. They were stuck in the same way as you. I wonder if we can all help to push you out and then maybe we can all do the same for Ronnie and Bett's car."

"That would work just fine." Roger said. He got into the driver's seat and we all pushed the motor home out of the mud easily.

"What do you call this Charlie?" Kathy asked as she grabbed a clump of moss and picked it up.

As I walked over to look at it, I said, "I call that a gold nugget." Everyone quickly came over and Roger got out too investigate what the fuss was. That mud that was churned up was loaded with moss and the gold nugget had gotten caught up in it, probably many years ago.

"That will easily pay for our trip home!" Roger exclaimed.

"That sounds good to me." Kathy said with a returning smile. Everyone laughed and we started up the dirt road to free Ronnie and Bett's car. That task was very easy with the large group of people we had with us. We all said goodbye to them and had a nice uneventful drive down the pass. We made a brief stop at Deckers for lunch and browsed around the river for awhile. We didn't find any more gold this day, but we did get to see a fly fisherman land a big trout before releasing it back into the South Platte River. When we got back to Colorado Springs, we were sad to see Roger, Carol and Kathy leave for home. There was something comforting about a lifetime memory with a happy ending.

CHAPTER TEN

The rest of that week went by ever so slowly. I was anxious for the arrival of Bruce and Jeanie from New York and the trip back to Forest City, which I was very much looking forward to. Mer and I, with Johnny and Flo, picked them up at the airport late Friday afternoon. We stopped for dinner at Flo's favorite Mexican restaurant in Manitou. Bruce and Jeanie were treated to their first real Mexican dinner, and they couldn't stop smiling. There is nothing as delightful to the taste buds as green chili and enchiladas. I especially liked the home made salsa, which will bring about a certain thirst for a cold beer.

When we arrived at our old Victorian style home near downtown, Bruce and Jeanie started unpacking in the spare bedroom upstairs. After just a few minutes, their senses started going crazy. I think Christiana was just saying hello. Jeanie came out into the hallway and yelled down the stairs, "Hey Charlie, we have a guest in our room!" I just laughed as Mer, Flo and Uncle Johnny giggled without end.

Our trip to Forest City the following day was everything I could have hoped for and more.

I had a surprise for everyone though. I had taken that week off of work and spent the entire time doing some intense research about the Reynolds Gang. Only

Mer had known all of the fun things I had learned, with the help of both a very knowledgeable librarian in the town of Fairplay, Colorado and a tucked away file folder in the Colorado Springs Library. I was able to make a large map with all of the events of the last week of July 1864 in the Park County and Platte alley. The file folder gave me the notes from a detective, Dave Cook, who investigated the Reynolds Gang robberies and hidden loot back in the late 1800's; he wrote a book in 1897. The librarian helped me to find the previous whereabouts of the Kenosha House. It had been moved since, but its previous location was ever so important in finding the location of the shootout and a clue to the hiding place of that stolen loot. The story board I had made up included dates and locations of events, as well as Detective Cook's hand drawn map of his best guess for the location of the loot. I sat down with everyone at the kitchen table after Bruce and Jeanie unpacked and laid it all out for them. This is the accounting I provided:

1. On July 24, 1864, seven Confederate renegades accompanied Jim and John Reynolds to Colorado from Texas. They had just robbed a train in New Mexico; it was said they got $48,000 in cash, arms, blankets, and a spy glass. They entered Colorado through Ca on City, then up to Park County through Hartsel. The first robbery was at Garand's ranch located between the towns of Hartsel and Fairplay. They stole $3,000 in cash and gold and another $1,200 from the passengers.

2. The gang moved on the Como where they robbed a Dan McGloughlin's Stage for about $10,000

3.   The gang then accosted a rich gold miner traveling in a buggy. H.H. DeMary was carrying just $100, which they stole together with his hat that one of the bad guys took a liking to.

4.   The gang went to Harriman's Kenosha House, (stage coach stop) near the top of Kenosha Pass. They robbed the occupants and may have molested the owner's wife.

5.   At about the same time, a passenger at the Michigan Stage stop, near Jefferson, set out on a journey through the Platte Canyon to warn the settlers. He was referred to as Mr. Berry.

6.   The gang went through the canyon following the north fork of the South Platte River, robbing everyone in sight.

7.   They stopped at Slaght's ranch in Shawnee for food and rest. No mention was made of a robbery.

8.   The gang showed up at the Omaha House at Schaeffer's Crossing near Conifer. Mister Berry was here at the same time and overheard the gang for a short time, and he said that they expected to be joined at Bergen's Park by other confederates to bring money for the Civil War. It was here that the gang found out about a posse coming after them from Denver. That was the direction that they were heading, but the posse changed their mind and direction. They went back in the direction from which they had

come the next morning. It was a Wednesday. They rode in the direction of Deer and Elk creeks. They were not seen for thirty hours.

9.   On Friday morning the gang sent word ahead to Slaght's ranch to prepare breakfast for them. After breakfast they mentioned always knowing where the posses were and disappeared again.

10. On July 30, 1884, a Saturday, a posse, led by Jack Sparks with twelve men, left Fairplay to warn the settlers at the Swan and Snake River settlements in the area of Guanella Pass. After dark, the posse spotted a campfire in a place Detective Cook described as a clearing in the trees, in the deep canyon down next to the north branch of the north fork of the South Platte about one and a quarter miles from the Kenosha House. The posse opened fire, killing a gang member named Singletary. The rest of the gang scattered into the brush. A Doctor Cooper from the posse cut his head off and was said to keep it in a jar in his office in Fairplay for many years after. The posse spent the night at the Kenosha House and returned to the spot of the shootout the next morning. There they found horses, saddle bags, gloves, muskets, traps, a spy glass, and some money together with one pack of amalgam gold. The posse supposed that the bandits all were carrying these packs of gold, but reckoned that they didn't have time to saddle up much of a treasure. They certainly left in a big hurry.

11.   An army posse captured five of the men near the Arkansas River near Pueblo and two more before they got back to New Mexico. One man was brought to Fairplay and gave the story of their wrongdoings there. The others were said to have been shot by an army private charged with guarding them. One of those men was Jim Reynolds, who kneeled down to be shot. He and his brother John were said to be very ugly persons. John Reynolds and a man named Jake escaped back to New Mexico.

12.   Years later an outlaw named Albert Brown gave a map and details of the hidden loot to Detective Cook. He had gotten the crudely drawn map, made with gun powder, from John Reynolds after he was shot stealing a horse. Before he died, Reynolds told Brown the following: When the posses got after them, he and Jim decided to bury the loot and split up until things cooled off. They took $60,000 in cash, wrapped in oil cloth and three cans of gold, weighing between twenty and forty pounds up the pass, which they thought was named Geneva Gulch. They went past a swampy area, in which one of the horses got bogged down and died. They then went up to the head of a creek he said was Deer Creek at about tree line. There they found a gold miner's hole dug in the ground and placed all the loot and covered the hole with rocks. They then stuck a butcher knife in a tree ten feet away and broke the handle off pointing at the hole. That was the same

day as the shootout. Albert Brown came to Colorado three times to find the loot but was unsuccessful. A forest fire had burned the trees and he could not find the knife in a tree or the hole. He did however find the horse bones in the swamp. Detective Cook never did look for the loot, but drew a map where he reckoned it might still be. He was sure that the Reynolds brothers had cached much of their money. While he was unsure of how much money they did have, he gave an estimate between $50,000 and $100,000.

Uncle Johnny was quick to come to a conclusion after I showed him where the head of Deer Creek was on a forestry map. He said, "Charlie that looks too far to travel on horseback in one day."

I agreed wholeheartedly. "Yes, I feel sure of it, although we can have a look today. I have found the original location of the Kenosha House with the help of a librarian in Fairplay. It does now sit at the entrance to Guanella pass and Geneva Gulch, but it wasn't there back then. This may be why so many people look for it at that location. John Reynolds did say it was Geneva Gulch, but there were no road signs then, and he was just there a few days without local friends. Back then there were lots of streams with the same name of Deer Creek. We can get to that spot and find the place of the shootout from there, one and a quarter miles distance. From that spot we should look for a swampy area, a creek and a tree line." Then we all packed into the van I had rented. The Jeep was too small for six people and Sarah.

We dropped little Mariah off on the way out of town at Cindi's house and day care center. She is just awesome with the kids and had our complete trust. As Mer started to take Mariah out of the child restraint seat, I cooed to her, as I always did, "Who's the prettiest and smartest girl in the whole world?"

She responded as always, "Riah is." We still have those conversations.

Then we headed up Ute pass as Bruce and Jeanie started to really enjoy their new found scenery. Ghost Town was on the left as we drove past Old Colorado City. A short distance later we could see Garden of the Gods rock formations, including the Kissing Camels, just before we passed Manitou Springs where the Pikes Peak Cog Railway ascends to the top of Pikes Peak. As the uphill climb begins we could see the Cave of the Winds and the Manitou Cliff Dwellings. Up ahead and past the swerving curves we spotted Santa's Workshop. Then we passed the sleepy mountain towns of Cascade, Bust and Green Mountain Falls before arriving in Woodland Park. All the while, the scenery was becoming more tremendous as we drove into the cotton candy like clouds. Turning south on Highway 67, the forest became less inhabited and more like the 19th century. We arrived at the town of Deckers, which is a cozy town sitting right at the South Platte River and is a favorite camping and fishing spot for locals. They brag about their big trout catches, which have always eluded my basket. Uncle Johnny was joke telling for most of the trip, including my experience of losing my biggest trout ever to a hungry eagle; okay, I may have embellished just a little—or maybe a lot. Although in my own defense, that eagle really did try for my trout at Skagway reservoir near Victor, Colorado—Jack Dempsey's and Lowell Thomas's home town and a now home to an operational gold mine.

As we arrived in Bailey, Colorado on Highway 285, we could see the roaring north fork of the South Platte River in the Platte Canyon below the mountain range known for the escape of the Reynolds Gang. Deer Creek and Elk Creek wash down the high range and trace the gang's footsteps in retreat from the posses. Anticipation grabbed hold of my thoughts and was duplicated by all in the van. As we discussed the possibilities of the true hiding place of the loot, I expressed my puzzlement about two unknown aspects of the history. When John Reynolds told Albert Brown the whereabouts of the buried money, how did he know for sure the names of the gulch and the creek? He had only been there a short time, and there certainly were no road signs. Also, there was the question of how far they could travel on horseback in the limited time that transpired between sightings. We drove past Shawnee, where Slaght's ranch no longer existed, but we could see the mountain range behind where they had breakfast that Friday morning. As we drove the distance to Grant-the entrance to Guanella Pass and Geneva Gulch-we knew that would have been a hard day's ride, but it may have possible. The Kenosha House was very visible there at the entrance. It was not there though in 1864. So we drove past it, and Jeanie blurted, "Charlie, that building has scary memories. I feel the screams."

Uncle Johnny had the directions I had given him as to the initial residence of that building. "Take that dirt road to the right Charlie, then stop at the cattle guard on the road. Okay, now look to the left, on the other side of that field. That is exactly where the Kenosha House stood." We were now about two miles up Kenosha Pass from the entrance to Geneva Gulch. "Okay, now we need to drive up this dirt road one and a quarter miles to the place of the shootout." Flo nodded as she looked over Uncle Johnny's shoulder, reading the words with him.

There was a swampy area to the left, but I knew that was not the one we were looking for where the horse got bogged down. "There is a little stream, Charlie. Didn't you mention something about the north branch of the north fork of the South Platte River?" Mer asked.

"Yes Mer, that stream passes through the 'deep canyon down' that Detective Cook mentioned, although I can only guess what he meant by that," I explained. We quickly found out what he meant. As we reached the mile mark, the walls of the canyon closed in; it was certainly at the lowest altitude in the canyon. We saw a sign that labeled this spot Hall's Valley. "That's it! The shootout happened just ahead!" I stopped the car exactly at one and a quarter miles on the odometer.

As we piled out of the van, Bruce looked in wonder and said, "This sure is the deep canyon down. I can almost hear the sounds of repeated gun fire." As we looked around, there appeared to be two logical spots for the actual campsite of the bad guys on either side of the road. To the right was a small clearing with large boulders that I was sure were there 130 years ago. To the left, the stream and a fireplace of stones were in an equally small clearing. We looked closely around that fireplace and found more modern discards than what we looked for. Also, there had been forest fires here. The trees were different now, and we couldn't assume the clearing was the same.

Jeanie stood fixated. "No Charlie, it is there to the right, between the boulders. The gang wanted that wall behind them for protection. I can see it now. It was a very dark summer night. The camp fire was raging.

Singletary yelled out. I hear horses. Just then, shots rang out in all out war. Singletary went down. Two other bad guys were wounded. The rest of the gang jumped on their horses and scrambled out through the pass we just drove in on. Then I see the posse returning here the next morning."

We all looked around the site, visualizing the gunfight-at least I was visualizing the gunfight. Mer broke the silence with the all important question, "Do you think that they buried the treasure in this canyon, Charlie?"

"It has to have been in this canyon or in Geneva Gulch. They didn't have time to go anywhere else. They could not have actually been at the head of the Deer Creek of today. That is at the top of Bandit Peak which is over 12,000 feet elevation. That is too high for tree line. I've got some forestry maps in my briefcase. I'll get them, and we can look at the layout of the mountain range up there that we can't get to," I trailed off as I ran to the van.

As I arranged the forestry maps, and we all began to study them and the time line, Bruce made a crucial observation. "We know they were here," pointing at Shawnee, "on Friday morning. They were chased up Deer Creek by the posse. They weren't seen again until Saturday night here, where we are standing. They could have gotten to Geneva Gulch by the end of the day Friday, if they were riding hard and didn't go to the top of Bandit Mountain. They could have gotten into Geneva Gulch using this trail." He said as he pointed at Rosalie Trail on the map.

"Okay", Uncle Johnny followed, "then, they could have buried the money in Geneva Gulch on Saturday morning, and then came here, or they could have come here on Saturday morning and just thought they were in Geneva Gulch. How could they know what gulch they were in without signs?"

Then Jeanie gave us the true benefit of her psychic intellect. "I sense that one of their members lived here before he joined the confederacy. I can see his face."

"Great Jeanie, that makes good sense. That would explain how the gang knew exactly where in Colorado to come find the gold miners. They made a bee line to this valley." I was relieved to solve that nagging inconsistency.

"If they did actually bury the loot in Geneva Gulch, why is there no Deer Creek there and how did they get over to Hall's Valley in half a day without going back out on the main trail, where the posses were sure to be," quizzed Uncle Johnny.

"They could have gone this way, couldn't they?" Flo asked as she pointed at the map.

"She is right! Burning Bear Trail goes right into Hall's Valley from the back of Geneva Gulch!" Uncle Johnny cheered and hugged Flo.

I scratched my head. "Okay, then we have one last, big puzzle to solve. If they weren't at the head of Deer Creek, what stream did they think was Deer Creek?"

We all stared at the map. Almost in unison, everyone smiled. "Geneva Creek must be the place!" Mer yelled. "The head of the creek is 11,209 feet. That is just below tree line. It flows on the other side of the mountain from Deer Creek. That must be why they thought they were still on Deer Creek, or it may have been called that back then." She stood with the poise of a geography professor.

Then I read the directions given to Albert Brown from John Reynolds. "You find the swampy area where one of our horses got mired down. Then follow Deer Creek up there a little ways, at about tree line. We buried the cash and gold in a hole dug by a gold miner on the side of the mountain. We then covered it with rocks and stuck a butcher knife in a tree about ten feet away. We broke the handle off of the knife pointing at the hole. Pay particular attention to my directions."

"I wonder why that Albert Brown didn't find the treasure after coming to Colorado three times?" asked Flo.

"I think I know the answer to that question, Flo," I smiled. "I don't know the year when Albert first came to Colorado. A forest fire could very well have burned that tree down, and the knife could very well have been buried in the ground. Also, the mountains erode by approximately one inch a year. That hole, which was covered in with rocks, must have new dirt covering it every year. Albert didn't have modern equipment, like metal detectors," I added like a cat that had just caught the mouse.

"But Charlie, that would mean that there could be 130 inches of dirt covering that hole!" Flo sounded flustered.

"No, I don't think so Flo. That hole is on the side of the mountain. Each year dirt would continue to wash down the side of the mountain. There may not be more than a foot or so, depending on the slope of the mountain," I confidently replied.

"Okay Charlie, let's buy that metal detector that you have always wanted," grinned Mer.

"Oh okay honey, if we have to."

"Oh Charlie, you sure do have great luck. Let's get up to Forest City and see how your luck is there," commanded Uncle Johnny.

"Wait Charlie, where is Sarah?" Mer asked.

We all looked quickly around. "Sarah! Sarah!" I yelled out. We heard barking, and then Sarah came running from the stream. "I guess she just needed a drink." I laughed.

As I opened the back of the motor home door for her, I noticed her left front paw was stained with something. I looked closer at the yellow spot. "Well, I'll be damned! Sarah found some gold!" Everyone came around the motor home to see the gold dust stuck in the fur of her paw.

"We had better look a little closer at that stream, Charlie." Uncle Johnny was already on his way as he anxiously pleaded.

"Okay, great, but I don't have my gold panning equipment with me," I replied dejectedly as we followed Sarah's foot prints back to the stream. As we looked closer, we could see an obvious pocket of black sand and gold dust in a tiny swirl behind a boulder on the inside of the stream.

Jeanie ran back to the motor home and grabbed an empty coffee cup. She sure was proud to scoop that gold into her cup. "Can I have this for a souvenir, Charlie?" she pleaded.

"Sure Jeanie, we wouldn't be here at this moment if you hadn't come to Colorado," I happily complied.

"There must be more gold in that stream," observed Bruce.

"Sure is Bruce. Now that I think about it, this mountain range is where the gold miners were getting their gold in the 1800's. It is also the drainage for the South Platte River. Gold hunters are still finding gold all over this river yet today. Also, the other side of this pass, in the direction we are heading, is where Dead Man's Gulch is. That is where we have been finding our nuggets. The Arkansas River goes through Park County over there too, and my Dad and I found gold in that river-as have many others. This whole region is the foundation for much of the gold coming out of Colorado. The Cripple Creek region is another," I informed him.

"Can we come back and get some more gold, Charlie?" Jeanie asked.

"Sure, let's stop back by here right after we pick up the Reynolds Gang treasure," I said as we all laughed

CHAPTER ELEVEN

We were all having such a great day as we traveled over the peak of Kenosha Pass. The view of South Park opened up and was just breath taking. We were all joking and laughing as we approached the town of Fairplay. Uncle Johnny was never without a laugh. "Hey Charlie, let's stop in at Doctor Cooper's office and have a look at Singletary's head," he joked.

As we drove further west toward Forest City, the van became quiet with the anticipation of all, except Sarah. She recognized the landscape and wanted out for a sniff as soon as possible. I pulled over at the first widening of the dirt road; Sarah got some sniff time, and we all decided to have a picnic on some nearby rocks. Roast beef sandwiches and cold beer were enjoyed by all, including Sarah. As a pair of falcons hunted from above, we could see a coyote sneaking past our picnic. The dark clouds were gathering quickly, as they often did in Colorado. Mer was a little worried about the weather. "Let's get going, Charlie. We don't want to get caught in a bad storm," her concern was apparent.

Uncle Johnny pulled the three pages from Kathleen Melanson's guest register out of his inside coat pocket and showed it to Bruce and Jeanie. Jeanie had an idea to read the other two pages. She got a small flashlight out of her purse and shined it on the pages from underneath them. "This one is a map Charlie. I'll trace it for us with this pencil. This second page is some writing. Oh, it is the written directions for the map. I'll trace that page too," said Jeanie calmly. Her excitement grew as she finished tracing the pages. "This map and these directions are to where we just came from. They are directions to exactly where we all thought the Reynolds Gang loot was buried. We were right, Charlie!"

We were so happy that the now full-fledged storm didn't bother us at all. As we got in to town, Mer spotted the Cheryl Dumas school house right away. "Oh, I have to go inside for a look, Charlie," she pleaded.

Everyone else wanted to go right into Kathleen Melanson's boarding house, so I let Sarah out and said, "Okay, I'll go with Mer. We'll meet you over there."

Then I let Sarah out, and she followed us into the little old west school. Mer opened the door and looked around in awe. "This looks so familiar, Charlie."

I replied, "Yes Mer, come to think-"

Just then, lighting, big and loud, struck close by. We were instantly transferred back in time. It happened just like the last time, except that Mer was with White Bear and me, and she was Maipaa now. Maipaa was astonished and just looked at me.

"Hi Ben, how have you doing Maipaa?" Cheryl Dumas walked toward us from her desk. "What a nice surprise, I didn't know that you were going to stop by today. What is the special occasion?"

"Is there any word of my brother, Daniel?" I quickly asked.

"No Ben, I'm sorry. There are many people out looking for him. Your brother Davy, Wyatt and Doc, the Pinkerton agents, and a special posse formed by the citizens committee are out looking as we speak."

"I have to leave this very minute, Maipaa. I have to go to the assistance of my brother," I spoke urgently.

"But Ben, you cannot get on a horse or ride with that bad foot. You can barely walk," responded Maipaa as she begged him not to go.

"I'll ask little Scott down at the stable to add a longer stirrup to the right side of a saddle. Then I could mount the horse from the opposite side just fine. I'll find Davy and the others as soon as possible. I have a very good idea where they are. Would that make you feel better?" I asked with a big please in my facial expression.

"Okay Ben, but be very careful. I expect you to become my husband." Maipaa's voice sounded stern; she was already good at that wifely duty.

"Wait Ben, I have something for you," Cheryl hurriedly said. She went to her desk and ran back over with a small derringer in a holster with an ankle strap. "Put this around your good ankle, Ben. It may give you some emergency protection. It was given to me by my father, who was also named Ben. So you see, it is very appropriate to give it to you. Besides, I don't want my children to be without their mayor just days after they got their first one," She added with a wink and a big smile.

Maipaa escorted me down to the livery stable and gave instructions to little Scott about how to tie that stirrup in the most secure way. "Okay, I'll do this properly, Ben. Let me pick out the horse for you," he requested. "You'll need a good mountain horse for climbing, and I have just the one for that purpose. He is smaller built and very sturdy. He is also short enough to make it easier for you to mount him." Scott began walking as he motioned for them to follow him.

Out behind the barn was the prettiest horse I had ever seen. He was a pinto with a beautiful long mane and fluffy tail. He gave me a soft push in my chest with his long snout. I took to him immediately and so did White Bear, who raised her paw to him in a big hello. "What shall I call him, Maipaa?"

"How about naming him Side Step, Ben?" Maipaa immediately responded.

"That couldn't be more perfect," I said with satisfaction.

Little Scott had him saddled in a jiffy, Maipaa and I had a long, long kiss goodbye, and in a second, White Bear, Side Step and I were galloping out of town.

CHAPTER TWELVE

It was early October now. The beautiful, yellow Aspen leaves were dancing and fluttering to the music of a slight fall breeze. The terrain on this path was familiar to me. I had first come to Forest City from Denver on this very same path. I would have to cross two mountain ranges to get to the Platte Canyon, where I thought Daniel and the others might be. The bad guys were probably there too. This way would save me a day in travel time, though. I knew the possible dangers ahead, and I was going over possibilities in my mind. The mountain lions and bears didn't have me too worried since I had White Bear with me. There were some rocky ledges to traverse, so I had to take care with Side Step. The bad guys were the scariest; I knew how sneaky and murderous they could be.

I double checked my saddle bag to be sure I had my binoculars with me. I was thinking I would need to keep a sharp eye up ahead. I needed to avoid those bad guys until I was in the company of my friends. But nonetheless, I was in an optimistic mood. My guts were pleading with me to relax. You have always had luck on your side, I told myself. It will turn out okay. Be alert, think well, don't panic in any event, I coached myself. White Bear and Side Step got along famously right from the beginning of our trip. They seemed to know what each other was going to do. First, Side Step would lead us on the path and then, without thought, White Bear would lead for a while. As the day turned into afternoon and we marched off the miles, that slight breeze had turned to a cold wind and the clouds darkened. Oh no, I thought. I hadn't considered an early mountain snow fall. Please don't do that, I thought in a plea to the Mother Nature. This was the Colorado Rocky Mountains though, and they always seem to march to their own tune. This day was no different. By late afternoon the flurries began. I had already been thinking about shelter for us all. I remembered that the valley we were about to enter contained an overhang of rocks on the side of a cliff. I was going to try to make tracks for there while there was still time. The snow came down faster. I was worried. The trail became blurry. White Bear led the way; she loved the snow.

Just then, I heard a voice, "Hey partner, where you headed?" I was relieved to see a friendly rider and then three more right behind him.

"I'm headed to the rock overhang in the valley for shelter," I quickly replied.

"Well stranger, you seem like an honorable guy to me. My name is Major Bruce Manning. This is my family." He motioned as the other three riders approached. "This is my wife Ilene and my two sons Joe and Mark."

"It is my pleasure to meet all of you." I quickly introduced my faithful companions. "These are my friends, White Bear and Side Step. My name is Ben Silver."

"Well, Mister Ben Silver, it is a real pleasure to meet a gentleman, such as yourself, on such a lonely trail." Ilene Manning spoke in such a graceful manner.

"Yes sir, how are you?" Joe followed.

"Can we help you, sir?" Mark chimed in.

"I would be grateful for some company and shelter in this storm we are about to endure," I responded as White Bear barked, pleading for us to get going.

Major Manning addressed me, "We are ranchers hereabouts, Ben. We came up to this place today to gather our cattle before the winter set in. Our ranch is a considerable distance, down Buena Vista way. However, we keep a cabin stocked with provisions not far from here exactly for occasions like this. We would be honored to have you join us for the evening. We can make a good dinner and feed your friends too." He tipped his hat in the direction of White Bear.

"Thank you Major. I would be delighted and grateful to except you kind offer." I was relieved to know I didn't have to wait this storm out in the elements.

"Then follow us," he commanded. They all turned and rode quickly towards the cabin. White Bear picked up the pace behind them, and Side Step was happy to keep up. On the way to the cabin, the snow stopped just as quickly as it began. The clouds cleared and the wind faded as it whistled its way down through the canyons and into the mountain prairie.

As we arrived, I was surprised at the quality of such a well built cabin so far away from civilization. The barn was fortified with sturdy timbers, so we quickly got the horses tucked in and fed with grain they kept in storage there. Side Step seemed especially satisfied.

As we entered the cabin, White Bear went directly to the bear skin rug in front of the fireplace and plopped down. She was content there for the evening. Major Manning started a fire, as Joe and Mark went out for more firewood; Ilene asked for my coat and went right into the kitchen area, started a fire in the stove, and got right to making dinner.

"Well Ben Silver, I sure hope you are hungry, because I have a great big dinner planned for my men. I am going to put some steaks on the fire with beans and my homemade biscuits. Also, I put a homemade apple pie in the cooling box just last evening."

"This sure is my lucky day," I said with a big smile. White Bear whined as if to say she was hungry too.

"Tell us why you are up here in this dangerous country Ben," insisted Major Manning.

As I told him the story of the bad guys, Ilene got a stern look on her face and said, "I saw three of those dastardly ruffians last week. They just gave me a nasty look when I asked them why they were on my land. Don't you worry Ben, you can count on us for any help you need with those devils. I am a pretty good shot with this here rifle," she insisted while showing me her prize gun.

Wow, I thought. She turned from a gracious lady to a ruffian very fast when right was met by wrong. Just then, shots rang out near. First one shot, then two more shots rang out. Then another shot which landed on something close by. Ilene ran out with her rifle still in hand. Major Manning ran behind, and I limped out to follow.

As she got out to the front porch, she exclaimed, "That rider is being shot at!" She yelled out to the rider, "This way, hurry!" Then another shot rang out in the direction of the rider. Ilene spotted the shooter on a nearby ridge just as I got out to the porch.

"Shoot him, Ilene!" The Major yelled out.

What happened then was befitting of only Annie Oakley. Ilene raised her rifle and fired without a hitch. I could see the snow ruffle as the shooter rolled down the mountainside. Then, I saw the rider. It was Maipaa. I shivered with the thought of the possibility of her being hurt. "Maipaa, Maipaa, over here!" I yelled out to her.

"You know her Ben?" the Major quizzed me.

"Yes, we are soon to be married," I responded. As Maipaa got down from her horse, I embraced her with a sense of relief I had never known before. "Are you alright?" I asked.

"Yes Ben, not a scratch," Maipaa answered.

"Are you crazy?" I asked her. "You could have been killed. Why did you come after me?"

"I had to warn you, Ben." She said with a gasp. "After you left, Bob the Baker, from the town of Epperson came to town with a delivery for Kathleen's boarding house. He warned us that he had seen that gang of murderer's that everyone has been talking about. He said that they were heading in the same direction in which you had gone. I wanted to keep you safe, Ben!" Her eyes did the rest of the pleading.

"I'm glad you're here, but I sure wish you would have taken someone with you for protection," I said with a deep breath, as I hugged her tightly.

"There was no time, Ben. I had to go fast," she sputtered.

"Can you introduce us, Ben?" asked Ilene.

"Sure thing sure shot," I chuckled with relief that she was that good with a gun. "This is my bride to be, Maipaa. Her name means peaceful water." Then I turned back to my loving messenger. "Maipaa, this is our new friend Dead Eye Ilene, her husband Major Bruce Manning and their sons, Joe and Mark."

After everyone said their hellos, Major Manning mused, "Well, I'd better take the boys up that hill and see if that villain is dead."

"Okay, Bruce, I'll take our guests in the cabin while I finish cooking dinner. When you guys get back, could you take care of Maipaa's horse,"

"I sure will honey," he complied.

I limped back into the cabin, happy to have Maipaa back under my arm. Ilene brought out a bottle of sipping whiskey to us. "Here you go. I think that I could use a shot too," she said taking a deep breath. "I always wanted to do that-kill a bad guy I mean."

"Well, I am very grateful, Ilene," replied Maipaa.

Major Manning and his sons came back into the cabin. "Well Ilene, he will not be shooting anyone else. He was dead right off. You shot him right through the heart! I am curious though, about why he wanted to shoot Maipaa?"

"He must be a part of the gang up here looking for the Reynolds Gang buried treasure," I answered. "They are shooting anyone who comes too close to the area of the buried loot. As a matter of fact, I think they have also been trying to scare off travelers as well. From what I have heard, there has been a headless horseman on the Phantom Trail. I have been thinking that this horseman is nothing more than one of the gang wearing a hood just to scare people away."

"Well Ben, we have to get our cattle back to the ranch tomorrow. When we get back there though, we would be happy to help you to corral those varmints," offered Major Manning.

"Thanks Major."

"I'd like to ask one question of you Ben, if you don't mind very much," added Major Manning.

"Sure Major, what can I tell you?"

"Do you have relatives from old Virginia? The reason I ask is because I heard about Sergeant Silver who killed three of our boys from the Northern Illinois

Regiment and then bragged about taking their mule prisoner. Was he related to you?"

"Yes sir! That was my father. I'm surprised that you heard about him."

"Your father was involved in the battle of Little Round Top at Gettysburg. I was an aide to General Buford. Our cavalry held the high ground in that horrible battle. Your father and his Confederate comrades almost flanked us at Little Round Top. If it weren't for the brave bayonet charge of Colonel Chamberlin, they surely would have done so and changed the fortunes of the battle and the whole damn civil war. Those three soldiers that your father defeated were the bravest and dumbest in our regiment. The corporal that reported the incident to me said that your father was the toughest Johnny Reb he had ever seen."

"Thanks Major; your side won the war, but I think that we all won because now men like you and I are on the same side," I said most emphatically.

The next morning Side Step, White Bear, Maipaa and I had to say goodbye to our new friends. We were very grateful for that and to Ilene for saving Maipaa's life. We rode off hoping to see them again.

CHAPTER THIRTEEN

The weather was much better this day. Happiness surrounded us, with the exception of a worry on my part about where the bad guys were and what they were up to. I forgot about that for the time being though, choosing instead to think about my lost brother and what was ahead for us. As we crossed the next mountain peak, I could see the Platte Canyon ahead and hear the crashing water of the South Platte River.

"Where are you heading for, Ben?" Maipaa asked gently.

"I want to get to Devil's Head Mountain, where Daniel was to meet the Pinkerton Detectives. I'd like to have a good view of the alley from up there. We can take a rest at the stream draining from the top."

"Sounds like a good plan, Ben," approved Maipaa.

White Bear seemed to know where we were going. She led us right to the spot at which I was aiming. Just before w got to the stream, she barked at us to take a break. Maipaa and I dismounted. Side Step got a quick drink, as did White Bear. Maipaa went to get lunch from her saddle bag, and I went to the stream to fill up our canteens. As I bent over, I heard two shots ring out with a deafening sound. They came from two different directions. Maipaa heard them too, and we both looked around quickly. I could see a man fall down from behind a boulder. At the same time I could see a circle of gun smoke coming from the direction of what appeared to be a cave at the top of a bluff. "Stay here Maipaa," I said while I drew my gun and climbed up on Side Step. "Go behind those rocks until I call for you."

"Ben, I am coming with you, please," Maipaa pleaded.

"Okay let's get going," I responded, seeing her already mounting her horse.

As we got up the hill to where the man was shot, we could see that he was one of the bad guys I had seen in Forest City. His rifle was still in his hand and the gun barrel was still hot. It was obvious that his shot towards me was errant after he had been hit by the other rifle. "Let's go see who shot him, Maipaa," I suggested.

We rode quickly to the cave where I had seen the smoke. As we got closer, I could see the figure of a man with a rifle. He had a cloth wrapped around his forehead. Then I saw him closer. It was Daniel! We had found him, and he had just saved my life! "Ben, you need to be a little more careful, little brother," he said with ease, while trying to roll a smoke.

"Daniel, where have you been? Everyone has been worried sick about you. We are all out looking for you. Davy, Wyatt, Doc, your pals from the Pinkerton Agency and others are all hereabouts somewhere," I told him.

"Well Ben, it's like this. I really don't know much of what has happened. I just woke up when I heard White Bear barking. Then I saw that rascal with a rifle pointing at you, got my gun, and let him have it. My head sure hurts though," he complained.

Maipaa went to him and commanded him to sit down. "Let me have a look at your head, Daniel."

"Okay, but be gentle will you."

"You have been grazed by a bullet, Daniel. You are very lucky to be alive," she informed him while cleaning and bandaging the wound.

Just then a stranger came around the rock corner. He was a mountain of a man. His stature was tall and muscular, with a face of serious business. "Are you all okay?" he said with a deep, strong voice.

"Yes, thanks to my brother Daniel here," I said looking over to Daniel. "Who are you?"

"My name is Dwight, Dwight Ringler. I was just over on the next hill when I heard the shots and came running. As for this fellow, you say he is your brother Daniel. He was ambushed by one of those rascals. I saw three of them get on their horses after I heard the shot that grazed his head. Then I carried him up here to my claim, put a bandage on his head and was waiting for him to wake up. I have been watching hereabouts for the gang of rascals that have been raising so much hell in this valley." He spoke with steel determination. "Who are all of you?" he asked with a sudden smile.

Daniel spoke up. "Thanks for coming to my rescue, Dwight. My name is Daniel Silver. This is my brother, Ben Silver and I think, his soon to be bride, Maipaa. I am a detective for the Pinkerton Agency. I was up this way looking for those murderous rebels. One of those gang members is a relative of John and Jim Reynolds, who led a gang of robbers hereabouts in 1864. They robbed many an honest gold miner and buried the stolen loot before getting their just rewards at the hands of a posse from Fairplay. I reckon they are after that buried loot."

"Well, that is exactly right," Dwight informed us. "I snuck up to their campfire the night before last and overheard their treacherous conversation. Those red legs have been wanting that loot to restart that damn Civil War. They plan to take that money to buy guns and go down to Alabama where they could get some recruits and try to start a new uprising. They are just plain crazy. One thing though, they are having a lot of trouble finding that loot. They can't find that knife in a tree or the gold miner's hole that the loot was said to be put in. I reckon it has been covered up by time."

"I hope they never find either," Maipaa interjected.

"Well, we still have a problem," I added with a pause. "They have been shooting people. They need to be arrested and tried in court. Also, the Department of the Army needs to be notified about the threat to reignite the Civil War," I followed in a matter of fact manner.

"I see our friends coming up the hill," Daniel said as he pointed down the hill at some riders.

"Sure enough Daniel. There is a sight for sore eyes," I said in relief.

Sheriff Kinney was first in line, followed by Davy, Wyatt, Doc and the Pinkerton Detectives, Matt Baker, Steve Clark and Nate Gang. Davy spoke first. "Daniel, it's damn good to see you brother. You had us a little worried. Although I knew that you could sure enough handle yourself in a fix. What the hell happened to your head?"

"It's just a graze Davy," Daniel smirked.

"Ben, how the hell did you get here before us? Are you a magician now as well as Mayor?" Davy looked puzzled.

"Must be that new fast horse I have Davy. Maipaa named him Side Step," I said with a twinkle in my eye.

"I'd say his name ought to be Fast Step," Davy said in disbelief.

"Who is your new friend?" Sheriff Kinney asked.

"This is Dwight Ringler," answered Daniel. "He carried me up this hill after I was shot and has taken care of me until I woke up to hear White Bear barking. That's when I had to settle up with that dirty rascal that shot me. Seems like he thought he could bag two Silvers when he was fixing to take a shot at Ben."

"Ben, don't you go and get yourself shot again. I don't think you have any more whiskey to pay for my operations." Doc laughed at his own joke.

After Wyatt chuckled a bit at Doc's joke, he asked, "What is it about you Silvers? It seems like everyone wants to be shooting you all."

"I don't know about that, but it sure is interesting to see how they keep surviving," Matt Baker mentioned as the other two Pinkerton agents, Steve and Nate, just shook their heads in disbelief.

"Why don't you get down for a well-needed rest?" Big Dwight suggested. "I'd like to tell you about what those murderers are planning. I've got some moonshine in my live-in cave here."

"That sounds real neighborly to me," Doc referred to the moonshine.

As Dwight talked about what he heard around the rascals' campfire, eyes became very wide. Matt Baker immediately spoke up. "I can't see any way around arresting those boys."

"I don't think they'll give up without a fight," chimed Daniel.

"You'll want to know one more thing," Dwight added. "They are expecting a group of reinforcements any day now from Texas way."

"Well, I think the ten of us can handle that mess of misfits," Sheriff Kinney said.

"What about me, sheriff?" Maipaa asked, not wanting to be left out.

"Maybe you could watch our back door, right here Maipaa, in case those reinforcements come this way." I pleaded with her to stay out of the melee.

"Okay Ben, just as long as I can help somehow," she agreed.

"Dwight, can you draw up the lay of the land where they are camped?" Davy asked.

"I most certainly will. Look here," Dwight said as he scratched in the dirt with his long bowie knife. "Those rascals picked a protected spot for their camp. At their back is a rock face wall going straight down. The canyon is narrow, just fifty feet, with a little stream passing through. The only way into the canyon is from the east or out of the canyon to the west. I was able to sneak up to their fire on a narrow weed patch on the other side of the stream. I figure if a few of us can get in there again, and then the rest of you troops get on both the entrance and exit paths, we'll have them cold," he said with the precision of an army commander.

"That sounds good to me, what about you guys?" Sheriff Kinney asked us all.

"I was just thinking," Maipaa mentioned with wide eyes. "We have some new friends in the canyon who are ranchers. The Manning family offered to help us if we needed it. If we can catch up to them while they are driving their cattle out of the canyon below, maybe we could-"

Daniel interrupted her before she finished her thought. "That is brilliant Maipaa! They could stampede the cattle through that safe canyon that those rascals are in, and we'll just wait for them on the other side, if there are any left!" He grinned that great big grin of his.

"We saw those folk just a mile from here on the way up the hill," Davy said. "I'll ride back down and see if they'll come on up here." Without delay, he got on his horse and rode away.

Dwight got out the promised refreshments, and Maipaa found some beans and bacon to cook for us. Davy quickly returned with the Manning family. The Major spoke first. "Hi Ben, your brother has told us about your plan. I want to tell you that we are all in on this plan to catch those scoundrels."

Ilene followed. "You bet Ben, my rifle is still ready for those ruffians."

Joe and Mark Manning both spoke in unison. "My rifle is yours too."

"Thank all of you." I was grateful to have so many new, good friends.

Sheriff Kinney asked Dwight, "What time of day can we catch those critters in their nest?"

Dwight answered, "Was late afternoon when they last returned."

"Major, how long will take to get the cattle down to Phantom Trail?" the Sheriff asked.

"We can have those cattle thundering through that canyon before sundown, Sheriff," he responded. "Will you all be ready?" he asked the sheriff back.

"Damn right, we'll be ready!" Doc quickly inserted, with the cup of moonshine resting on his lip. Everyone laughed.

The Major followed, "If you take Sundown Trail over there to the west, then you will all come down into the back side of that canyon in perfect position."

Dwight added, "There will be tree groves on either side of the canyon trail. I think that we can set up right there and post ourselves on the ready for those varmints."

While we were having a lunch, a loud noise of racing riders could be heard from the valley below.

Matt Baker quickly looked out of the cave dwelling. "It's those reinforcements!"

"Well that's good news to me!" Wyatt interjected. "We can catch all of the rats in the same trap!"

"That works for me," Daniel smiled.

"How many were there, Matt?" Davy asked, with a look of concern showing.

"It looked like close to thirty more rats," answered Matt.

"As I look around me, I think they are the ones that are outnumbered," Big Dwight assured them, "especially if we count the cattle."

After he stopped laughing, Daniel followed, "Ben, there will be no need for Maipaa to keep watch for those rascals now. I am thinking that she might accompany you up to the top of that rocky wall with your rifles and cover our backs from up there."

"Good thought Daniel. We'll be ready," I assured him. Then, we all saddled up to go out and spring our trap.

CHAPTER FOURTEEN

We got to the back side of the canyon in good time. It was well before sundown, and the wind was blowing up now. I was thinking that the wind whipping through the canyon would hide the sound of the cattle. Sheriff Kinney set up on the south side of the canyon with Matt Baker, Steve Clark, and Nate Gang; on the north side of the canyon, Daniel, Davy, Dwight, Wyatt, and Doc readied themselves. I spotted a trail to the top of that rock faced wall, and Maipaa and I headed up there with White Bear accompanying us.

"Keep a sharp eye, Ben," said Davy as we rode away.

"You can count on us," I replied with confidence.

As Maipaa and I dismounted and took our positions in a spot custom made for our trap, I looked below to see the gang gathering. Our view was like that of an eagle on his hunt.

Pretty soon, far in the distance, we could see the Manning's moving close to the canyon entrance. I looked to the west and saw our self-appointed posse lurching by the tree lines.

Most of the bad guys were all getting comfortable around a newly started campfire. There was a separate group though, having a private conversation in a secluded corner of the rock formation out of view from the others. I was wondering what they were up to and hoping they would break it up in time for our noose to be tightened. I counted six men in my view; there could be more that I didn't see. I waited for them to move to the camp fire with their dastardly brothers. I said to Maipaa, "That group will be protected from the stampede in that corner that they are in."

"What should we do, Ben?" She asked with worry.

"We have to do something. If they are still there for the stampede, they can pick off the Manning family as they go by." Just then I had a crazy idea, as I do on occasion. "Stay down."

"What are you doing, Ben?" she whispered back with her eyes growing wider.

"It will be okay, just stay down," I whispered back.

Then I stood up quickly, with my guns drawn and yelled down to the smaller group of bad guys. "You are all under arrest! Put up your hands, and get over there with your friends!" They all broke out into a big laughter, as did the other group of bad guys. It worked though, as they all moved together in one big group and were having a great time.

"We sure are afraid, hombre," one of the bad guys joked, as more laughs bellowed out.

"As the Mayor of Forest City, I am placing you all under arrest this very minute," I said with a straight face.

"Do you have enough hand cuffs for all of us bad guys?" he joked back.

I began to reply, "I'll shoot the first man who-"

Just then, the Mannings fired shots to start the stampede. The bad guys were in total panic. They scattered every which way, but had no place to go, except west out of the canyon. Some got to their horses. Others were trampled by the hard-running steers. I ducked down next to Maipaa and watched as the battle ensued. As the bad guys on horses got to the two groves of trees, the good guys came out with guns blazing. It was just like the shootout at the O.K. Corral all over again, except on a much greater scale. There were the Pinkerton's lined up on the left and Davy, Daniel, Dwight, Doc and Wyatt on the right. They were raising hell with those pistols and rifles. The bad guys were dropping so quickly, there was no counting them.

Then I saw two bad guys getting around behind Davy, I shot one quickly and Davy turned around to finish off the other. By now, the cattle had done their job, and the Mannings came in a shooting hard action. All four Mannings hit their first targets, then Ilene got another for good measure. They gathered up the mangled and wounded who had given up. Though by the tree groves, guns were rapid fire now. The good guys and the bad guys were head to head and face to face. Matt Baker took a hit and went down. Steve Clark did the same to the bad guy that shot Matt. Dwight got four before he went down wounded. Davy and Daniel made me proud. They were out shooting a lot of twelve or more. Wyatt and Doc were doing the same to an equal number. The bad guys left retreated on foot to a rock enclave. Dwight got up with a wounded shoulder, went to his horse and grabbed a few sticks of dynamite from his saddle bag. He looked over at Doc and grinned, "My right arm is still good, Doc. Can you hit these?"

One of the bad guys, seeing the dynamite aimed at Dwight. Daniel shot him dead, dead, dead. Dwight threw the first stick of dynamite. It landed within ten feet of the bad guys. Doc immediately hit it with the first bullet. The explosion got three of them. "That will be one shot you owe me, Dwight!" he yelled over.

"Try this one for double or nothing," Dwight said with a smile. The other good guys were smiling too by now. He threw another and then a third. Doc hit them both with perfect measure. The bad guys were obliterated. The fight was over. As we all gathered, and the Mannings brought their prisoners limping over to the tree groves, five in all, we all took a sigh of relief. Maipaa bandaged Big Dwight, and Steve and Nate carried over the body of Matt.

Daniel took off his hat and said, "This brave man had no family. We are his family. He fought for us, and we fought for him. We will never forget our brother Matt Baker."

"What do you want us to do with the bodies of the bad guys?" Wyatt asked Sheriff Kinney.

The Sheriff replied, "I'll wire the US Marshal's office when we get back. You brave souls can share in the bounty."

"What about these here prisoners?" asked Major Manning.

"Let's hog tie those rats and get them to the Forest City jail. I'll have the Marshal pick those varmints up too," Sheriff Kinney said with a deep breath.

"Dwight, we need to get you to a Doctor!" I exclaimed.

Then Doc interrupted, "Ben, have you forgotten me so soon?" Then he looked over at Dwight with a smile and said, "Care to make that a whole bottle of whiskey?"

"As long as it's quick," Dwight replied, knowing what was coming next.

Doc said, "It'll be quick." Sure enough, he had that bullet out in no time at all. We all said goodbye to the brave Manning family, as they were set to gather up their cattle and head toward Buena Vista. Before they left though, Maipaa and I asked them all to be at our wedding over at Bret and Bonnie G's ranch. They agreed to meet us there as soon as they got their cattle penned up. When we rode out of that canyon, Daniel looked over at me with a grin and said, "Ben, if you ever do another crazy stunt like you did back there again, I'll shoot you myself."

Davy added with sarcasm, "I'll do the same, Ben."

I smiled at both and said, "Now, you brothers of mine know that I never do crazy things." Then I looked over at Dwight and said, "Why not come with us to Forest City to heal up and come to our wedding."

"That sounds just great to me little brother. I am family now, aren't I?" Dwight replied with that mountain of a man kind of smile.

"Darn right you are!"

Davy echoed my sentiments. "Darn right." Then Daniel agreed saying the same thing.

We all laughed with great cheer through the valley. Just before dark we were looking for a place to make a camp fire when we heard a horse ride up. To our surprise it was Kathleen Melanson. "What are you doing out here by yourself?" I asked her.

"Now Mayor Ben Silver, I'll be reminding you for the last time not to be getting yourself killed. We have a good town, with good people, and you need to be taking care of us. Joe Hensmith, the editor of *The Mountaineer*, got a telegram from the Denver Pinkerton agency. They said to let you know that US Marshals would be coming to your assistance. Now you darn well know that I can take care of myself, so here I am," she told me matter of fact.

"Oh, well thanks Kathleen," I humbly replied.

Then she looked over at Dwight with an unusual twinkle in her eye and said, "Now, what have you done to this poor little guy?"

"This is Dwight Ringler. He has been saving our butts since we met him,"

"Well, mister savior Dwight, I am Kathleen Melanson. Now sit down, and let me have a look at that shoulder." Kathleen motioned to a nearby rock. It seemed like they made that rock their home for quite a while, if you know what I mean.

The next morning we woke early and headed toward Forest City, thinking about what a fun wedding we were going to have. Sheriff Kinney had a big smile on his face dragging those prisoners along. Daniel and Davy said goodbye to us at Kenosha Pass. They said they would join us at Bret and Bonnie G's ranch in a few days. They wanted to go down to Denver for something, although they wouldn't say exactly what. Wyatt and Doc headed for a quick stop at Leadville. They had a hankering for a game of cards. They said that they would also meet us at the ranch, and Doc reminded Dwight about that bottle of whiskey which was owed. Steve and Nate stayed with the Sheriff, Dwight, Kathleen, Maipaa, and I to be sure the prisoners didn't act up. White Bear and Side Step knew the way back and took turns leading us back to Forest City. When we got back into town by the end of that day, the Marshals from Denver were waiting outside the jail house and quickly took charge of the prisoners.

Maipaa dismounted and walked quickly toward two people standing outside the saloon. "Cherie! Is that you?"

"Yes Maipaa, I sure missed you," Cherie replied back. "Let me introduce you to my fianc , Bradley Paul, Just call him Brad."

"I'm very pleased to meet you Brad," Maipaa said with her outreached hand.

"It's great to meet you Maipaa. Cherie has told me so much about her best friend. I feel like I already know you." Brad smiled as he reached out with his big hand to shake with Maipaa.

"Come here Ben," Maipaa requested of me. As I went over to them, she said, "Ben, this is my best friend ever, Cherie Patton and her fianc , Brad Paul." I shook hands with Brad and Cherie and expressed my affectionate hello. "Ben is the Mayor of Forest City," beamed Maipaa.

Then Maipaa turned back to Cherie. "You are getting married too! Ben and I are to be married in just a few days."

"Oh, that is wonderful!" Cherie jumped for joy.

"How did you get back here?" Maipaa asked her.

"Well, while I was home in Missouri, my dad sent me to a finishing school. Brad is a builder by trade, and I met him there while he was building a new teacher's home. I have just finished school, and Brad wanted to come west and build homes for all of the settlers coming west. I suggested Colorado because I was so familiar with it after having spent so much time here when Mom and Dad left me at Kathleen's Boarding House with you last year, while they traveled to Santa Fe. When we got to Colorado Springs, we heard about the wagon train that just came up to Forest City, and I told Brad that this would be a perfect place for us."

"Oh Cherie, Cherie, I just had a good idea!" Maipaa clapped her hands in excitement.

"What, what, what do you mean?" Cherie asked in a playful way, which I learned was standard for her fun personality.

"Why not get married together? I mean at the same ceremony. It would just be great. Ben and I have already made arrangements to have a wedding at a ranch nearby!" Maipaa said with great joy.

"Oh yes, we must do that," Cherie replied. Then she turned to Brad and asked, "Would that be okay with you, honey?"

He smiled like a Minnesota gentleman and replied, "Yes! I feel at home already."

Maipaa turned to me and asked, "Ben, can we please?"

"Absolutely! I think that would be terrific!" Seeing Maipaa so happy made my heart jump in my chest.

"Ben can we all get married on the 17th, Friday, 3 days from now?" Maipaa asked.

"Sure, if it's okay with Brad and Cherie, and, of course, if it's okay with Bret and his family,"

"That sounds great to me." added Cherie.

"That sounds great to me too," Brad followed.

Cherie and Maipaa hugged. Then Maipaa asked Cherie and Brad, "Will you be staying at Kathleen's?"

"Yes, for the time being," Brad responded matter of fact.

"Can we help you get settled in?" I asked. We all started towards Kathleen's with big smiles all around. When we got to the boarding house, Kathleen gave a big hug to Cherie and all introductions were made. We all retired to our rooms.

The next morning, as I looked out the window, the streets were buzzing when all the local folks began to hear about the big shootout with the young Reynolds Gang. Big Dwight sat out on the front porch with Kathleen, telling Scott and Clyde about his aim with the dynamite sticks and Doc's eagle eye shooting. Sheriff Kinney relayed all the other details to the Citizens Committee. Cheryl Dumas was hanging a sign on the front of the school house. It read. 'There will be no school on Friday. Everyone is invited to a joint wedding ceremony!'

"Gosh Maipaa, the word has sure gotten out quick about the wedding," I said in surprise.

"I confess Ben. I whispered in Kathleen's ear before we came upstairs. She whispered back to leave it all up to her and Debra Montana to take care of the details," smiled Maipaa. I just laughed in relief, knowing my worries were over for now. After breakfast, I asked Brad to go with me to *The Mountaineer* and ask Joe Hensmith to get word to Davy and Daniel in Denver about the date of the wedding and also to see if Doc and Wyatt could get away from their poker game in Leadville. While we were there, I introduced Brad to Joe and asked Joe to put a notice in the next edition of his newspaper about Brad's ability to help the new settlers build their dream houses. That got a big smile from Brad. That is when Maipaa and Cherie came running in all excited. "Ben, we must all go down to St. Louis Sue's new cottage. She has offered to make our dresses and your suits for the wedding. She must have measurements straight away," Maipaa beckoned.

"Okay, Maipaa, but we need to find out if Friday is a good day for Bret and his family to have a wedding."

"Oh Ben, Debra Montana has already sent riders over there this very morning. Steve Clark and Nate Gang volunteered and left at sunup," Maipaa said as if to say just relax.

By the end of that day, it seemed like all of the arrangements had been made. Steve and Nate returned with a note from Bret that they would be delighted to have the wedding on Friday. Steve mentioned that Bonnie was preparing a feast for the ages. We made a plan to go over to Bret's ranch on Thursday after Sue had finished her needle work, which she did in fine fashion. Maipaa and Cherie went out to pick wildflowers before we left and also got a special flower for White Bear to wear at the wedding.

The trip to the ranch was very uneventful as trips went for us. The weather was beautiful, and when we arrived everyone was busy putting up decorations. Bonnie G showed us to our rooms and filled us in about all the details. The ranch was a perfect place for a wedding. Bret had already built a Gazebo and sent for Preacher Owen Anderson to come and officiate.

The next morning, everyone was very cheerful and busy. Bonnie G and Bonnie and Sarina were working quickly in the kitchen. People were arriving with good cheer. Doc and Wyatt made it to the ranch in time from Leadville. Davy and Daniel arrived from Denver with big smiles on their faces and a special envelope carrying a wedding present for Maipaa and me. They explained how they had gone to Denver and purchased a lovely piece of land from a rancher that Davy had known. It was 320 acres of the best land just west of Forest City. "Oh, that was your surprise!" I exclaimed. "Wow, wow!"

Then came Kathleen with Big Dwight in tow and Cheryl with all of her school children and husband Ron. The wagons behind them were filled with many dishes that Kathleen and Debra had requested and a special present of their own. They brought four identical gold wedding bands which were hastily, but nicely, made by the town goldsmith Ted Anders. They also brought with them a handful of musicians and Kellie Repute for the entertainment. Kathleen explained that little Scott had ridden to the town of Boulder to solicit her attendance. She was happy to comply and glad to see Daniel. Also, at the very last minute, the Manning family rode in. They were told about the wedding by Doc and Wyatt on their way from Leadville.

When the sun was high in the sky and everyone was ready, Maipaa and I, with Brad and Cherie, walked through the assembled and clapping crowd and assumed our places on the gazebo with Owen. His words were very touching and appropriate. We said "I do's" with a tear in our eye, and the tears flowed in the crowd as well. We were pronounced men and wives, and the celebration began! Dinner was served among the beautiful aspen trees. The music commenced immediately after and lasted into the night. The golden beer was plentiful as was the good cheers by all. It was a wedding to behold and remember.

The next morning was very quiet when Maipaa and I awoke. Something was wrong though. I looked over at Maipaa and she looked back at me with blurry eyes. We were both fading, and then as quickly as we had come to this time, we were gone from it. We awoke with Uncle Johnny, Flo, Bruce and Jeanie looking over us.

"Are you sleeping on the job again, Charlie?" Uncle Johnny asked me with that big, gotcha grin of his.

"You wouldn't believe it if I told you," I said with a smile back.

"I would Charlie. I sure would," Jeanie assured me as if she knew everything.

"I would believe it too Charlie," Bruce added with a wink.

"Well, let's get home," I pleaded. "We have to get a metal detector and get to work finding that Reynolds Gang treasure." Sarah was a little hard to wake up, but we got her going and off we went down the Mosquito Mountain Range.

We didn't get too far before Flo made an offer we couldn't refuse. She said, "My restaurant isn't too far away, Charlie. Why not let me treat everyone to dinner? I have some nice Buffalo steaks in the freezer and some of your favorite green chili. I also have a special treat for Sarah." That rang a bell for Sarah, who responded with two of her well known barks. Everyone else definitely liked the idea, too.

"You are on, Flo," I confirmed. That was an awesome meal and lots of laughs for everyone, compliments of Uncle Johnny. Then we continued our trip down Ute Pass thinking about a treasure hunt that we were all anxiously awaiting.

CHAPTER FIFTEEN

The following day was a Sunday. Bruce and Jeanie wanted to see Old Colorado City and Manitou. So, we loaded everyone into the van, and this time little Riah got to go. Old Colorado City was a territorial seat in the 1800's and, you might say, a little rough and tumble. Manitou was a place for a mining exchange when the golden years of Cripple Creek were in full swing. Now though, they are the cat's meow for tourists and locals alike. We enjoyed breakfast on the patio at Bon Ton's Caf at the foot of Pikes Peak and drove up and around Gold Camp Road. The view from the top is awesome and comes down by Helen Hunt Falls, where we stopped for an afternoon picnic. We also stopped in at the awesome view at Seven Falls. Then, we drove around the famous Broadmoor Hotel to the Cheyenne Mountain Zoo and finally a stop at the Will Rogers Shrine. I think the high altitude tired Bruce and Jeanie out, as they needed a nap. So, I took advantage of some free time and drove down to the library to double check all my research. When I came home, Mer could see that there was something wrong. Flo and Uncle Johnny were sitting on the couch, and Bruce and Jeanie had just wandered down the stairs. Sarah was being teased by Riah with a mechanical puppy. "What is the matter Charlie, you look like you just saw another ghost?" She asked as everyone looked over at me.

"I am stressed and worried," I replied.

"What are you worried about Charlie?"

"I just found another file folder at the library, which I had not seen before. There was an article I read that suggested that Detective Cook may not have been accurate in his recollection of events about the Reynolds Gang. For instance he said that he was with the posse from Denver, but the directions that he gave to the Platte Canyon from Denver was over the Kenosha Pass. That pass is at the end of the canyon on the way to Fairplay," I explained.

"Oh, that's nothing Charlie. I often forget how I got somewhere, myself," Uncle Johnny inserted with a chuckle.

"Okay, you are right, but we are relying on part of his story as to where the treasure might be buried," I expressed with much concern.

Jeanie reassured me, "Charlie, my sense is that you are right on target."

"Okay, but there was one other thing I found out: John Reynolds escaped with a bandit named Jake and maybe one more of the outlaws. He and Jim buried the money and gold. Jim was shot by an army guard on the way to Fort Lyons. So Jim was the only person alive to know where the money was buried. He was said to be a gambler in New Mexico for a while and then may have come back to Colorado in 1871. If he did come back, why would he not dig up the treasure?" I asked.

"But Charlie, he certainly wouldn't have given a map to a friend and sent him on wild goose chases after his death," Mer suggested. "Also Charlie, you and I know, after what we just went through, wink, wink, that his only son John was after that same treasure in 1886," she followed with a smile.

Flo settled it all. "Charlie, the research you have collected may or may not be all true. Who could ever verify these facts? The fact is that we are having an awesome time on this treasure hunt, find it or not." Everyone else followed with some let's go get it cheers.

"Okay then," I sighed with assurance, "I guess what we should do is go on over to a special gold panning supply company, that I just happen to know about, and get that metal detector." And did we ever get a good one. It was the most powerful model in stock and could also discern gold in the ground.

"Charlie, I think we had better stop off at Dead Man's Gulch for another nugget to help you pay for that," Uncle Johnny suggested.

"Well, that's a good idea. But, you know, I think there could be lots of gold where we are going," I said with renewed enthusiasm.

"Charlie, we are going to find some gold. I know it," Bruce assured.

Before the sun came up the next morning, Sarah took her place in front of the door. She always knew when a trip was coming. I packed the van while everyone was getting their coffee, and we took a sleeping Riah over to Grandma and Grandpa's. What would we ever have done without Grandma and Grandpa? We were already at the city above the clouds-Woodland Park-by daybreak. We were all getting anxious as we approached the Platte Valley. Uncle Johnny made sure we weren't without laughs though. He told the story to Bruce and Jeanie about how he saved my life from a grizzly bear with his Swiss army knife. Then he demonstrated with his serious look, "C'mon, I'll cut you to pieces!" He couldn't stay serious long, as he quickly laughed.

The water was running slowly this time of year; I thought this was good for us. We could take a few samples in the stream on the way up the mountain. It was quiet now, as we entered Guanella Pass on the way into Geneva Gulch. There was the swampy area to the left. We couldn't know if that was the place that a horse had gotten bogged down in with the Reynolds Gang, but it was a good sign. We saw the stream also off to the left, which we hoped was the one John Reynolds referred to as Deer Creek. "If that stream crosses this road off to the right and comes from the top of that mountain, we might be on to something," I said holding my breath.

Then there was quiet as we observed the incredible awe of the Rocky Mountains. On for a while we drove, then, "That's it, Charlie! Up ahead, it crosses the dirt road!" Uncle Johnny yelled with a whoop-de-doo.

I spotted a nice parking place for the van, and we all got out with anticipation. Sarah was jumping for joy. We divided up the supplies for each to carry. Uncle Johnny always volunteered for the heaviest load, which of course was the cooler of refreshments. Bruce and Jeanie took the gold pans and bottles for gold. Flo took the most important lunch cooler, I took the shovels and pick ax, and Mer took the metal detector. "Which side of the stream should we go up on guys?" I asked.

"It's simple Charlie. Horses couldn't make it up that other side with all those rocks. It's a sure bet the Reynolds brothers went to the left," Bruce said most assuredly.

"Okay, well we had better get started. I think we are about 9,500 feet elevation. According to my forestry map, we have to climb up to over 11,100 feet, close to tree line."

"Is your bad ankle going to be okay for that climb Charlie?" Mer asked me with that look of concern a good wife can sometimes get.

"Sure it's just a hop, skip and a jump," I said with a smile. We started up through the bright yellow aspen trees. It was a beautiful autumn day. Birds were all about. Sarah scared off a pair of mule deer. We could hear the light breeze fly through the trees. We could hear something else too; this noise was not as comforting. It was an animal for sure. It was making a snorting noise from the ridge above us. The girls looked at each other, and we men did the same.

We walked carefully now alongside the stream. Uncle Johnny, Bruce and I watched intensely along the ridge. Then we saw it. Uncle Johnny started laughing first. Bruce and I followed his lead with a bellow before the girls realized what we were laughing at. It was a rutting elk, making his wishes known with those big snorts. We all laughed so hard, we had to sit down and take a break. Sarah barked and jumped in the air as if to join in on the laugh. We were all relaxed now that the danger was over. Just then, boom, crash, bang. All hell broke loose around us. Something was in chase of that daddy elk, and it was big, and it was mad. It was so quick we didn't know exactly what it was. Looked like a bear, but no bear ever ran like this, on two feet. It screamed as if to say something. We saw it for just a second or two. "Wow, what the hell was that?" Uncle Johnny asked in surprise.

"Ah, it was nothing," Bruce said calmly. "Every race of beings on earth has its share of freaks. That there Bigfoot is just another freak of nature."

"Oh, Bruce is right," Jeanie reflected. "Let's get going."

We all chuckled at the ease that they had handled their first scary Colorado moment. Mer and I knew that these beings existed and didn't mean any harm to people. Uncle Johnny and Flo also took it as just another treasure hunt experience. None of us separately would admit to a stranger of this sighting, but together, we all knew.

Then, we heard a yell from above the Aspen trees below. "What is going on up there?" a man's voice asked.

"We aren't really sure," I yelled back. Then through a clearing in the trees, I saw a familiar silhouette. It was the frame of a hero I had previously known. He was my savior at Dead Man's Gulch.

"Ranger Myron Garrison, how are you! Remember me, Charlie?"

"Oh sure Charlie, how could I forget you? Are you in trouble again?" He asked with his familiar what's-he-up-to laugh.

"Well, I'm not sure yet. There was a bit of a strange happening just a minute ago. Something was chasing a bull elk up across that ridge. Now, we think we know what we saw, but we are not sure that we know what we think we saw," I said as his look became puzzled.

"Well, I know what I saw Charlie. I don't think it is a good idea for any of us to swear to it. Why are you all up here on this dangerous ground?" the ranger asked with concern. Before I could answer, he said, "Wait don't tell me, I think I know. You're treasure hunting again, aren't you?"

"Yes, you sure do have my number," I confessed.

"Well, it looks like you have a good crew of miners Charlie," The ranger observed as he smiled at everyone. "You wouldn't be looking for that Reynolds Gang treasure, would you?"

"How did you know that?"

"People have been looking for that for a hundred years," he said. "Some of our rangers keep an eye out for that knife stuck in a tree, pointing at where it is buried. Most people think it is on the other side of that mountain though, at the head of Dear Creek and near the head of Elk Creek. You must have been doing some more research."

"Yes, indeed I have. We think that we have good reason to believe that it may be near here. What brings you up here, Ranger Garrison?" I asked.

"The Forest Service has a crew of people up here, mapping the old gold miner holes. We have been working on that all summer. I am just double checking whether or not we found them all," he informed us.

"Oh, well I guess you already have a treasure map?" I asked in wonder.

"I wish I did Charlie. I would sure enough give it to you. I don't think that we have mapped that particular hole, or I would have known about it. These locations on the map are mostly larger digs that are a hazard to hikers. I don't imagine that those Reynolds brothers would have chosen such a big hole as a hiding place."

"No, I suppose not," I replied. "But, I am curious about how much erosion would have covered up those holes. I have learned that these mountains erode by one inch a year."

"Yes, I think that is about right. But, don't forget that the sides of the mountains are eroding downhill too, at a rate depending upon the degree of slope. Some holes on a deep slope have actually washed away." That is when my bell rang, Uncle Johnny's too.

"Well Charlie, maybe we should look downhill for our treasure," he said with a smirk.

"Maybe you should," the ranger added with a smile. "Well, I have some work to do. Charlie, I do hope that you stay clear of any escaped convicts today. Good luck to you all." The ranger walked back into the flickering aspens.

"What do you think Charlie?" Mer asked. "Could that money and gold have washed away long ago?"

"It's possible and maybe even very likely. Do you all want to continue our search?" I asked everyone.

"We sure do Charlie," Bruce added as Jeanie nodded her head. "I hear that you have had some very good luck over the years."

"Yah Charlie let's go for it," Flo added.

"Maybe Mer should keep that metal detector on as we go up the hill, Charlie," Uncle Johnny recommended.

"Okay, now you're talking. Sarah, lead the way," I commanded.

She responded with a chorus of barks, as she bounded up the side of the stream. Uncle Johnny whistled a tune for us as we climbed higher and higher. I had an overwhelming desire to stop at the stream for a gold sampling, but, like everyone else, I wanted to get to the head of the stream and look for that glory hole. It was quiet now. The water ran so slowly, we could barely hear it. At about halfway to tree line, Bruce spotted a small entrance to a gold mine. As we walked toward it, we spotted a sign at the entrance. It read: 'Dangerous-DO NOT ENTER.' We took that advice easily and moved on further. The stream turned to the right and led into a pool below a small waterfall.

"Wait a minute, let's think about this," I pondered. "Could those brothers have thought that this is the head of the creek?"

"It's possible Charlie. I can see the tree line up there," Bruce observed.

"Oh look at the pretty wild flowers Charlie," Mer said as she set down the metal detector to go pick a few. Mer never lost her Mer, no matter where she was. That is exactly when it went off; the metal detector was humming like crazy. Everyone ran over to it. "What did I do, what did I do?" Mer asked in astonishment.

"Exactly what we wanted you to do," I said with a smile. "Find something without trying. That is what happened in Dead Man's Gulch, remember?"

"I sure do, Charlie," Uncle Johnny said with amazement.

"I remember too," Flo laughed. I picked up the metal detector quickly and tried to get an exact spot for the alert. As I moved it in a circle the signal got weaker and then stronger. I pinpointed the spot, and Bruce dug in with the shovel. About eight inches down, the shovel hit a piece of rotting wood.

"Whatever it is, it must be under the wood," Jeanie commented.

Uncle Johnny said, "Wait a minute," as he bent down to pull the wood out. "It's stuck." He grimaced to pull it out. It seemed to be stuck to something. Then Bruce dug a wider hole and hit something metal with the shovel.

"That's not gold," he said in dismay.

Then I looked at the settings on the metal detector. It was accidentally set to discern all metals. "It's set for all. That could be anything; let's see what it is anyway." Bruce continued digging deeper and around.

"Eureka!" Uncle Johnny yelled. "It's the knife Charlie, can you believe it!" We all looked wide-eyed as he pulled a rusted old knife blade out of the rotting piece of wood.

"That sure enough is a knife blade," I commented. "But, can we be sure that is the knife that the Reynolds brothers stuck in a tree to point at the miner's open hole?"

"Charlie, my psychic whispers are telling me that is exactly the knife that we were looking for," Jeanie said with confidence.

"Okay, if we assume that it is, where was the tree that it was stuck in to? That piece of rotting wood must have been part of that tree," I asked out loud.

"One thing is for sure," Uncle Johnny said, "The glory hole is somewhere between right here and that tree line, right there." Everyone took a deep breath. The realization of that statement was very reassuring.

"My guts are telling me it is around that pool somewhere," I said. "I think that those guys thought the pool is the head of the stream and not where the water comes out of the ground."

"Good thought Charlie. Let me try that metal detector," Bruce said as he took it and started hunting around. Uncle Johnny and I thought this was a good time for a beer and a sandwich.

"How can you be thinking about a beer right now, Charlie?" Mer asked.

"That helps us think better." Uncle Johnny laughed.

"Yah honey; it's time for reflection," I said with a smile. Sarah barked in agreement as she put her paw up for her own share of lunch. Bruce went all around the pool with the metal detector and didn't even get a buzz, so we all took a lunch break.

"Oh look at the cute little black squirrels," Mer observed as two squirrels chased each other around a moss covered embankment.

As I looked over at the moss, I had a thought. "The Reynolds brothers buried the treasure at the end of

July. The water level would have been much higher that time of year. We need to look above that spot with the metal detector."

"Let me have a turn," Flo demanded, reaching for the metal detector. She walked directly above that embankment and immediately the metal detector went off. It was really screaming. We all ran up, and Bruce grabbed a shovel. As he dug, he immediately hit a rock. He pulled it out and then hit another, and another. The rocks were the size of basketballs and there were six in all. We all knew what this could mean and took a collective deep breath. Just then, Bruce pulled out something we had hoped for but not exactly what we expected.

"Well, look here. What do we think that this is?" Bruce quizzed himself.

"It's an old metal can," Mer said. "What's that stuff all over it?" she asked looking as she just tasted castor oil.

Uncle Johnny grabbed hold of the can and pulled a rotting piece of oil cloth out, which had been stuffed inside. When he opened up the cloth, he found a leather one pocket type wallet. "Who wants to open this?" he said as if we were all at the moment of truth.

"Let Mer do it," I requested.

"Okay Charlie, I'll do it," she said most assuredly. As she opened the wallet, her face had a look of confusion on it. "It's a piece of paper. No wait, it has writing on it." As she opened it up a gold coin fell out onto the ground.

Jeanie picked it up and said. "It's a twenty dollar gold coin. It was minted in 1861."

"That actually could be worth a lot of money," I said. "What does the note say, Mer?"

"Well, it looks like I can read it," she responded. "It says, 'If yuse is one of dem looking for the stolen loot, I beat you to it. Ha, ha, ha. My name is Joe, won't tell ya my last name. I dug this here hole last year lookin for gold. Wasn't no gold here. When I came back here this June month, 1865, I saw that this here hole that I dug was buried wit these here rocks. Heard about those Reynolds rascals, I did. Figured something was amiss. Unburied it I did, got me over sixty thousand cash money and two cans o' gold. This here can is one of dem. Yuse can have da can, I'll keep the loot. Ha, ha, ha. But, I'll leav ya dis here coin for your truble so yuse don't cry too much. Ha, ha, ha.'"

We all just looked at each other, stunned. Then Uncle Johnny started laughing louder than I have ever heard him laugh. We all joined in. It was very funny. Good for Joe. Jeanie held up that coin though and wondered, "Hey guys, what is an 1863 twenty dollar gold piece worth, these days?" with a great big grin.

"That coin is probably thousands of dollars, these days," I said as my world grew considerably brighter.

"Well, let's sell it and go on the sight-seeing trip of our life, while Bruce and Jeanie are still in town," Mer suggested with a cheerful face. Everyone quickly agreed to that. We finished our lunch and reflected on a great achievement. After all, we did find the famous hiding place of the Reynolds Gang loot. That guy Joe deserved to find it first. He was the guy up on that dangerous mountain, putting his life at risk everyday in the harshness of the old west. Also, that nanny-nanny-boo-boo laugh he got with the note, really was very funny.

"Hey everyone, we have to make a stop at Forest City," I suggested.

"What for Charlie, do you need another nap?" Uncle Johnny joked.

"No, I am not tired at all. I just thought that we could pick up that 1886 penny that I left in the horse post over a hundred years ago," I said with a big smile. No one knew what to say to that except Maipaa-I mean Mer.

"Trust him, it is there," Mer said with confidence. Sarah barked all the way down the mountain. We all laughed and joked as if reinvigorated by our treasure hunt.

"Charlie, it's a good thing that I didn't have to fight off that Bigfoot with my Swiss army knife," Uncle Johnny quipped.

"I don't think he would have dared mess with you, Uncle Johnny," I quipped back.

"I had my shovel ready," Bruce assured us.

"I would have been standing behind Bruce," Jeanie added.

"I would have run as fast as I could," Flo joked.

"I would have hid behind Sarah." Mer was not kidding.

Sarah seemed to sense our conversation making a "grrrrr" noise.

That following week was the most fun that any of us had ever had. We toured the Front Range of Colorado, ate at the best restaurants, and drove through the best scenery that you could ever imagine.

Mer and I have both had beautiful dreams about our 1886 wedding with all our friends. We remembered having a beautiful young daughter named Miriam and watching her grow up riding all of her little ponies. I wondered about why I had not found an article about my brother Daniel until I went by the library and found it misfiled behind Davy's obituary.

Mer and I were sitting out on the gazebo yesterday, while Mariah was out catching butterflies. Mer asked me a very serious question. "Charlie, could you please just wait a few weeks before you go off chasing another treasure. I don't know if you need the rest, but I sure do!"

I just laughed, and said, "Okay honey." I try not to argue with her when she is right.

I added one thing though. "Mer, I think that our next adventure might just be a treasure to die for.

"Oh Charlie, the only treasure in life worth dying for is the treasure we have in friends and family." Mer said with that big picture intelligence she has always had.